The past twenty-four hours had felt very strange, and yet very right.

At times it had almost seemed as though they were a real couple, decorating their place for Christmas.

Except for the constant reminder that their relationship was transient. That she shouldn't get used to spending time with him when he could be gone again before she knew it.

Saying goodbye to Duke was going to be torture.

As the afternoon waned and the light dimmed slightly, Duke went inside and flicked the switch to the outdoor plug, making the lights come alive.

It was beautiful.

Duke came back outside and jogged down the steps, coming to stand beside her. "So what do you think?" he asked. "We did good, huh?"

Her breath made clouds in the air, and Duke tugged on her hand, pulling her closer.

He kissed her, slow and soft, making her melt against him. The man knew how to kiss—she'd give him that.

"Whew," she said when the kiss broke off. "I'm not sure the fun's quite over, you keep kissing me like that."

His eyes warmed. "It doesn't have to be."

Dear Reader,

Welcome to a brand-new trilogy—and just in time for the holidays!

In the Crooked Valley Ranch series, you meet the Duggan siblings: Duke, Lacey and Rylan. None of them are ranchers, so it's a bit of a shock when they inherit the family spread from their grandfather. Each of them must take their place at the ranch or it goes up for sale.

Which doesn't really matter much to any of them...in the beginning. In *The Cowboy's Christmas Gift,* Duke Duggan returns to the ranch to figure out what to do next with his life. A career soldier, he's at loose ends now that he's lost his hearing in one ear. At first he just wants to get his bearings. Look at his options. It all sounds great until two things complicate his "no commitments" plans. First of all, he kind of likes the ranch and the open spaces and freedom. And then there's Carrie Coulter, the cattle foreman. Smart, feisty and loyal, she keeps Duke on his toes. Duke's torn between his freedom, wanting to reunite his family for Christmas, and knowing that selling the ranch might have devastating consequences for those who count on it for their livelihoods. That's a lot of responsibility for one guy to shoulder.

Good thing Duke loves a challenge.

I hope you have a wonderful family holiday and enjoy the warmth of the season—as well as a good book or two!

Best wishes,

Donna

THE COWBOY'S CHRISTMAS GIFT

—

DONNA ALWARD

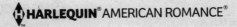
HARLEQUIN® AMERICAN ROMANCE®

Recycling programs
for this product may
not exist in your area.

ISBN-13: 978-0-373-75545-5

The Cowboy's Christmas Gift

Copyright © 2014 by Donna Alward

All rights reserved. Except for use in any review, the reproduction or
utilization of this work in whole or in part in any form by any electronic,
mechanical or other means, now known or hereinafter invented, including
xerography, photocopying and recording, or in any information storage
or retrieval system, is forbidden without the written permission of the
publisher, Harlequin Enterprises Limited, 225 Duncan Mill Road,
Don Mills, Ontario M3B 3K9, Canada.

This is a work of fiction. Names, characters, places and incidents are
either the product of the author's imagination or are used fictitiously,
and any resemblance to actual persons, living or dead, business
establishments, events or locales is entirely coincidental.

This edition published by arrangement with Harlequin Books S.A.

For questions and comments about the quality of this book,
please contact us at CustomerService@Harlequin.com.

® and TM are trademarks of Harlequin Enterprises Limited or its
corporate affiliates. Trademarks indicated with ® are registered in the
United States Patent and Trademark Office, the Canadian Intellectual
Property Office and in other countries.

Printed in U.S.A.

ABOUT THE AUTHOR

A busy wife and mother of three (two daughters and the family dog), Donna Alward believes hers is the best job in the world: a combination of stay-at-home mom and romance novelist. An avid reader since childhood, Donna has always made up her own stories. She completed her arts degree in English literature in 1994, but it wasn't until 2001 that she penned her first full-length novel and found herself hooked on writing romance. In 2006 she sold her first manuscript, and now writes warm, emotional stories for Harlequin.

In her new home office in Nova Scotia, Donna loves being back on the east coast of Canada after nearly twelve years in Alberta, where her career began, writing about cowboys and the West. Donna's debut romance, *Hired by the Cowboy,* was awarded a Booksellers' Best Award in 2008 for Best Traditional Romance.

With the Atlantic Ocean only minutes from her doorstep, Donna has found a fresh take on life and promises even more great romances in the near future!

Donna loves to hear from readers. You can contact her through her website, www.donnaalward.com, or follow @DonnaAlward on Twitter.

Books by Donna Alward

HARLEQUIN AMERICAN ROMANCE

HARLEQUIN ROMANCE

*Cadence Creek Cowboys
**The Texas Rodeo Barons

Other titles by this author available in ebook format.

To Kate Hardy, with many thanks for all the help and words of wisdom!

Chapter One

Duke Duggan turned the slightly battered half-ton up the dirt drive to Crooked Valley Ranch. Whorls of dust swirled behind him, clouding the frosty road as he made his way to the ranch house he remembered from childhood. It hadn't changed a bit. The white siding and dark green window trim was definitely dated, but the wraparound porch he'd always loved still skirted the house, making it welcoming and cozy-looking.

Or it would look cozy if not for the brown grass and nearly naked trees. November was a pretty bleak month—past the glorious splendor of fall colors but before the blanket of pure white snow that would soon fall in the small ranching town of Gibson, Montana.

Nerves twisted in his stomach. This homecoming hadn't been in his plans. The letter from his grandfather, sent via the old man's lawyer, was tucked securely in the breast pocket of his denim jacket.

Duke had still been in the hospital overseas when his grandfather had died, and he wished he'd been here to go to the funeral. Despite the tensions between them, Joe had still been family, and Duke had spent a good part of his early childhood at Crooked Valley Ranch. Those had been the years when his dad had still been alive, and as time passed, it felt to Duke as if the memories were slipping further and further away. He worried that sooner or later they'd disappear altogether.

That time hadn't come yet, though. He clearly remembered the rolling hills in the shadow of the mountains, waving grass, horses and cows dotting the verdant pastures, and a bedroom decorated with rodeo wallpaper—his dad's old room. His dad had taught him how to ride a horse before he rode a bike, and it was something he'd always enjoyed during the times he'd spent at his grandparents' place.

Duke also remembered arguments between his mother and his grandparents, Joe and Eileen—particularly after his dad had died. Mom had never loved the ranch, and her mother-in-law and father-in-law had known it. Something Duke did remember clearly was his mother repeating that she only stayed at Crooked Valley because Evan had wished it while he was deployed.

Sgt. Evan Duggan—Duke's father and hero.

Duke had only been eight when his dad was killed in Iraq. Twenty-two years ago now. With no further reason to keep her promise, Mom had moved them away from Crooked Valley and the small town of Gibson to Helena, where she took a government job and supported them all. Duke, along with his sister, Lacey, and brother, Rylan, only saw their grandparents occasionally after that. A week in the summer, and maybe once or twice during the year on holidays. Once they were teenagers and more concerned with friends and part-time jobs, they saw the Duggans even less.

Duke had liked the time he spent there in the summer. He'd been able to ride every day, hang out with the hands, most of who had known his dad as a kid, too. They'd shared stories with him that helped Duke feel closer to his father—a man Duke really couldn't remember all that well beyond a shock of red hair, a big smile and a uniform.

He'd liked it here, sure. What kid wouldn't enjoy the freedom of the great outdoors? But that was a far cry from wanting to be a rancher himself. Especially when he wasn't consulted and part ownership was just thrown in his lap, piled on top of his other worries. He didn't want the ranch to fall into a stranger's hands, but that didn't mean he and his siblings were equipped to step in. No sirree. He knew how to be a soldier. He'd been damned good at it. He didn't know anything about ranching.

One-third of this tired-looking ranch was his—if he wanted it. Trouble was, Duke didn't really know what he wanted—other than a good dose of peace and quiet. Maybe the odd chance to blow off a little steam once in a while. Time to figure out what was next for him, because he'd only been home for two weeks and he had no idea what he was going to do for the rest of his life. He was out of the army and, without it, he wasn't sure *who* he was at all.

Duke slowed the truck as he reached the sprawling yard that contained the house, several outbuildings in need of paint and shrubs that looked as if they hadn't seen a trimmer all summer. He frowned. It didn't look like the prosperous, well-tended ranch he remembered. Maybe he'd be better off going back to Helena and bunking in with Ricky Spencer. Spence had given Duke a place to sleep and an offer of a job at his auto repair shop after Duke had left the army behind.

Except working with Spence would just be a Band-Aid solution. He sighed. This probably would be, too. But maybe, once he'd been here for a few months, he'd have a better idea about the future. Like what he wanted to do about it. He was a soldier, period. Except he wasn't, unless he wanted to be a desk jockey. Without a doubt he knew he'd go crazy doing that. With his hearing loss being permanent, his options were more limited than they used to be.

He felt like a puppet, at the mercy of whoever was pulling the strings.

Duke parked the truck next to the biggest barn, the one where he remembered disappearing to each day in the summer to spend time with the horses. He got out and stretched his arms over his head. The weak autumn sun felt good, though it did little to warm him. The air was clear and fresh, though. He let out a big breath, a cloud forming in front of his face. What did feel right since returning home was the big Montana sky, the sun, the smell of the air. There was nothing like it in the world—and he'd seen a lot of places.

Birds chirped in the skeleton branches of the scrub brush, but Duke had a problem telling where the tweets and burbles were coming from. Losing half his hearing had been a blow, but at least he could still hear out of his left ear, and he still had all his fingers and toes. That was what he kept telling himself anyway. The gash on his arm had healed to a pink scar and so had the bruises. But the hearing loss was permanent. He was damned lucky he hadn't been killed by the IED and he knew it. That didn't mean there weren't adjustments that he had to make. Or that he deeply resented having to make them.

"Hey! I said, can I help you!"

Startled, he spun to his right to see a man, much smaller than himself, marching toward him from the back of the barn. He squinted and realized it was no man at all—it was a woman, in jeans, dirty boots, a denim jacket similar to his own and a battered brown hat on her head. The words she'd hurled at him echoed in his head. *I said, can I help you!* Clearly they'd been spoken more than once and he hadn't heard. He clenched his teeth, annoyed at his disability once more.

"Jeez, I called out three times. What are you, deaf?"

He raised a surprised eyebrow as the words hit their mark. "Wow. That was rude."

She huffed out a sigh as she came close enough he could see her face. "Bad morning. Sorry."

He looked closer. "I'll be damned. Carrie? Carrie Coulter?"

Blue eyes looked up into his. "That's right. And you are?"

It only took a half second after the words were out of her mouth for who he was to register. "Oh, my God. Duke Duggan?"

He hadn't seen Carrie since what, third grade? Back then she'd had a space between her front teeth and freckles, and sandy blond hair that she always wore in a perky ponytail with pieces sticking out at her temples. Once he'd called her Freckle Face and she'd kicked him in the shin so hard he'd had the bruise for two solid weeks.

She still had the same pieces of hair sticking out and curling by her hat brim and the same freckles, too, only they were a little bit lighter now and the space was gone from her teeth as she gaped up at him, mouth open. Huh. Carrie Coulter had turned out quite attractive when all was said and done, even dressed in dirty jeans and a bulky jacket that didn't do her figure any favors.

"Well," she finally said softly. "I think hell just froze over. Didn't think you'd ever make it back here."

"Why not?"

He watched her lips as she answered. They were very fine lips, full and pink without even a touch of gloss or lipstick. "Your grandfather always wanted you kids to come back and you never did." Her eyes took on an accusing look. "I think it broke his heart."

"His heart broke when my dad died," Duke stated dispassionately. "Don't get me wrong. I liked my time here as a kid, but after Desert Storm..." He frowned down at her. "It was always about my dad. Wanting us to take over the place since my dad never would."

Duke had heard it so many times as a kid, how his father had failed the family. It was no wonder that Duke had rebelled against the idea of joining the ranch, instead determined to honor his father by following in *his* footsteps and joining the army. But it hadn't only been about rebellion. Duke had wanted to be a soldier and he didn't regret that move in the least. Not even considering his injuries. He'd served his country and done it proudly. It was all he'd ever really wanted to do.

"You didn't hear how much he talked about you," she replied, a little tartly, he noticed. Clearly Carrie had been devoted to the old man.

"You knew him better than I did."

"My point exactly. What are you doing here, Dustin?"

She was mad. That had to be the only reason she reverted to his real name. He'd been Duke for so long that he was surprised anyone would even remember that his birth certificate said Dustin. It felt as though she was addressing a stranger.

He made a point of hooking his thumb in a careless gesture, motioning toward the back of the truck where two duffels sat side by side. "I'm here. As one-third owner of Crooked Valley Ranch." To prove it, he took the letter out of his breast pocket and handed it to her, ignoring the slight feeling of panic he got just saying the words.

She opened it, walked away a few steps as she read the words. Words that had caused several reactions within him when he'd opened the envelope. Anger, grief and, strangely enough, fear. After all the places he'd been, things he'd seen, danger he'd been in, it was the idea of taking over Crooked Valley that made him most afraid.

He could tell she said something because he heard the muffled sound of her voice, but couldn't make out the words. He turned and took a few steps through the crackly grass until he was facing her again. "I beg your pardon?" he asked.

She held up the letter. "I had no idea. When Joe died, I asked Quinn what we were supposed to do and he said keep working until we heard differently from the lawyers. When did you get this?"

"Last week," he confirmed.

"And your brother and sister?"

He shrugged. "I don't know, I haven't talked to them lately. They have commitments. I don't. Not at the moment anyway."

She folded the paper and handed it back to him. "Well, I have to say I'm a bit relieved. We've all been wondering what was going to happen with the ranch. But what about the army? Are you just on leave, or what?"

It stung more than a little to have to respond, "The army's in the past. By the way, who's Quinn?"

There. He'd changed the subject. He'd rather not talk about the circumstances around his leaving his former life. It was still too fresh.

"Quinn Solomon. The ranch manager."

"And you're what, a ranch hand?" He couldn't help but smile a little at the idea. Most of the girls he knew wouldn't be caught dead with manure on their boots, dirt on their face and less-than-perfect hair. It seemed impossible that the cute little girl he'd teased in school was now working on his ranch. That would make her his employee....

All traces of friendliness disappeared from her face. "No sir," she corrected him. "Quinn's the manager, and I'm the foreman of the cattle side of the business. And if you'll excuse me, I've got to get back to work. We lost two heifers to coyotes last night. I need to bury the bodies."

Bury the bodies? Coyotes and heifers?

Duke had had visions of riding the range, surveying his domain, moving cattle from pasture to pasture and some sort of idyllic, carefree life for a few months while he made some hard decisions. That vision hadn't included predators and dead bodies and digging graves. That wasn't his idea of stress relief. He'd had enough of that sort of thing during his deployments.

"You need some help?" he asked, knowing he couldn't send her out there to tackle it alone.

She turned back to face him, which made it easier for him to understand her next words. "I've got a couple of hands who'll help me. Why don't you go get settled? You'd only get in the way anyway."

She strode off before he could form a suitable reply. Okay, so he was a greenhorn. He admitted it. But he was part owner of this ranch and she worked for him now, even if it was a formality. Her dismissive tone definitely grated on his nerves.

He turned away, hopped back into the truck and

drove over to the main house. Once he figured out where he was going to stay, he'd deal with Carrie Coulter and her uppity attitude.

CARRIE'S HEART BEAT against her ribs the whole way back to her ATV.

She'd wondered what Joe's plans for the ranch were. Wondered if she'd find herself out of a job and left with a mountain of bills still to pay and a winter's worth of heating to come out of her bank account. It was an enormous relief to know that she still had employment and that she'd be able to keep the wolf from the door. And a pain in the ass to find that her new boss didn't know ranching from his armpit. Duke Duggan had always had too high an opinion of himself in school. He'd grinned and teased and called her Freckle Face and pulled her ponytail. She remembered. It had been a relief when he moved away. Sort of.

And my, hadn't he grown up. She tugged on a pair of gloves, swung her leg over the seat of the quad and fired up the engine. She gave the throttle a shot of gas that sent her lurching away from the barn and toward the twin tracks leading down the hillside to where the herd was grazing. She couldn't banish the memory of his deep blue eyes staring down at her in surprise, or the intent way he watched her face as she spoke. Never mind he was now at least six feet tall and, from the looks of it, all lean muscle. His hair was military-short and had looked naked without a hat. If it grew out, she imagined it would be a rich auburn, not quite brown and not quite red.

Son of a…

She bounced over a hard rut and gripped the handlebars tighter. Why the hell should she care what color his hair was anyway?

If she was lucky, Duke would spend most of his time with Quinn. Quinn was the real boss here, overseeing most of the ranch operations, especially once Joe had gotten older and his health had declined. Duke could stay out of her way and just let her do her job. She had enough to worry about. Like paying off her mom's medical bills. The estate hadn't covered the expense and now, two years after the funeral, Carrie was finally seeing the light at the end of the tunnel. Maybe in another year she could stop scrimping and saving quite so much as she got out from under the debt.

Worrying about money wasn't going to solve the current problem, though. She had cattle to take care of... and a coyote problem to solve. She was just thankful that Duke was here to take over, no matter how annoying she found him on a personal level. Someone needed to take responsibility for the ranch. It wasn't the perfect situation, but it was better than nothing.

"COME ON, CARRIE." Kailey Brandt fell back onto the bed with her arms outstretched. "It's Friday night. And I don't want to go to the Wooden Nickel alone."

Carrie tried not to laugh. The Wooden Nickel was the nickname Kailey had given the Silver Dollar Saloon, saying a dollar was far more than the old bar was worth. "I'm tired. I had a busy week," she answered.

"Didn't we all," Kailey replied, undaunted. "Girl, you've been wrangling cows and coyotes. You need to blow off some steam. Have a beer. Flirt with a good-looking cowboy and have a dance or two. Maybe some mattress mambo."

Now Carrie did laugh. "You just want to see if Colt's going to be there."

Kailey turned her head away and the grin slid from her face. "Colt Black can dry up and blow away for all I care."

Carrie sat down on the bed beside her friend. She and Kailey were close, both being farm girls at heart. Kailey was in charge of the bucking stock over at the nearby Brandt place, and they were both used to working in a physically demanding, male-dominated industry. Once in a while they got together and decided to feel like girls for a few hours. Friday nights at the saloon usually fit the bill.

"What happened between the two of you?" Last Carrie had heard, Colt's gaze had been fixed on Kailey just as much as hers was on him. The last time they'd been in a room together, Carrie had been certain she could light a fire with the hot looks passing between the two.

"I waited too long. He hooked up with some girl from Great Falls with big hair and bigger boobs." Kailey looked down at her ample but not overly huge chest. "What is it with guys and breasts?"

Carrie laughed again. Kailey was like a breath of fresh air.

"Please, Car." Kailey stared up at Carrie with big blue eyes. "If you don't, I'll end up spending Friday night at home with the old folks watching Thanksgiving Hallmark movies on TV." She shuddered.

"Oh, all right. But I'm not staying late. I'm dog-tired, Kailey." Never mind she'd spent the past few days trying to stay out of Duke's way. Their paths had only crossed a few times since their initial meeting, and he'd been engrossed in conversation with Quinn, just as she'd wanted it.

So why had she felt so disappointed when he hadn't answered her hello, but merely nodded and kept walking?

Because she was a damned fool, that was why. Truth was, everything she held dear was tied up in Crooked Valley Ranch. The fact that Duke had showed up had been nothing short of a blessing. He could be as crotchety as he liked, as long as he kept Crooked Valley running and her in a job.

She straightened her shoulders. "I guess I should get dressed, then. And put on some makeup."

Kailey sat up. "That's the spirit! You should wear that red shirt with the V-neck. And I'll fishtail your hair. You've got way better hair than I have for that. The braid makes your summer sun streaks stand out."

And so it was that less than an hour later, both girls walked into the Silver Dollar. It was busy already, and they had to wait for one of the tables on the perimeter of the scarred dance floor. The Dollar had once been an old barn that Cy Williamson had renovated. Right now the latest country hits echoed to the rafters, along with lots of chatter and laughter.

Carrie took off her coat and tugged at the neckline of her shirt. She'd let Kailey steamroll her and now felt conspicuous at the little bit of cleavage revealed by the V. She was wearing makeup, too, eye shadow and a bit of liner and mascara and lipstick, of all things.

Scott Johnson was staring over at their table and Carrie gave Kailey a kick. "You're getting attention already. Jerkwad Johnson at two o'clock."

"Oh, for Pete's sake." Kailey forced a smile. "Let's get a beer and forget he's there. First round's on me."

Kailey got up and went to the bar rather than waiting for one of the waitresses to make her way over. Carrie watched as several eyes fixed on her friend's attractive figure as she leaned against the old wooden bar to give her order. She wondered if Kailey really knew how beautiful she was. No matter how dolled up Carrie got, when she was with Kailey she always felt a bit like the ugly stepsister—without the bad temperament.

The double doors opened again and Carrie froze.

In walked Quinn Solomon—he must have got a sitter for his daughter tonight—and Mr. Prodigal Grandson himself, Duke Duggan. Jumpin' Judas, the man was good-looking. He smiled at something Quinn said and it made his face light up. His jeans fit his lean body just right and he wore a brown coat with a sheepskin collar that made his shoulders look impossibly broad. His boots were clean but not new, and he'd hidden his buzz-cut look beneath a brown hat.

Mercy.

Kailey returned to the table and put down two bottles of beer. "Mother McCree, who is that?" she asked, nudging Carrie's arm with the cold bottle. "Whoo-eee."

"My new boss," Carrie replied drily, blindly reaching for the bottle. "Duke Duggan."

"What? No way. I don't remember him looking like *that*."

"He was eight when he moved away," Carrie reminded her. "You were six. Your memory might be a little foggy."

"Right. Well. This changes the evening significantly."

There was no reason on earth that Kailey's words should inspire a flicker of jealousy, but they did. It was ridiculous. Carrie didn't like Duke and had absolutely no claim on him. Why should she care if Kailey was interested?

As if he could feel their eyes watching him, he turned their way. She could tell when he looked at Kailey, because his eyes twinkled a little and he raised an eyebrow just a bit.

But then he looked directly at Carrie and her breath froze in her chest. The twinkle disappeared from his eyes, but they remained warm, and a smile touched his mouth. And then he lifted a finger and touched the brim of his hat before turning away and following Quinn to the bar.

Her breath came out in a hot rush. Oh, man. She was in big, big trouble. He was her boss. He was a pain in the butt. And he made her pulse race in a way it hadn't in a very, very long time.

Chapter Two

Carrie was starting to feel as if her buddy had forsaken her. It was Kailey's turn to drive, so after the first drink Kailey switched to cola and stayed there. They always took turns when they went out so one of them was a designated driver. It was their way of looking out for each other—the best sort of buddy system.

Except not only had Kailey coughed up the cash for the second round, she'd made sure that Carrie's drink was a very stiff rum and cola, and then moved their seats closer to the other side of the bar—and closer to Duke.

The hard liquor on the heels of the beer already had her feeling a bit fuzzy, and it seemed as if without even trying she could hear Duke's voice, deep and gravelly as he talked to a group of ranchers nearby. She tried not to look his way but couldn't help it. She was intrigued. After their rough start the other day, she'd spent some time thinking about what his life had been like after he'd left Crooked Valley. She couldn't imagine being taken away from the wide-open ranch land to the confined space of the city, but he had. He'd gone to city schools and not the K-12 school in Gibson, which only had one class for each grade. He'd visited here in the summers but not for years, and then he'd gone into the military. One thing she noticed was that while he was talking right along to Quinn and a few other local ranchers, he didn't smile much. And he didn't laugh.

In fact, Duke looked pretty darn somber as he focused intently on the conversation. Way too serious for a Friday night in a saloon with cold drinks and good boot-thumpin' music.

"Do you suppose he realizes you're staring at him?" Kailey asked.

"What?" Carrie turned back to her friend and felt her cheeks heat. "I wasn't staring."

"Sweetie, you know I don't like to call you a liar, but…you're a liar."

"I wasn't staring." She looked Kailey dead in the eye. "Much."

Kailey laughed, and sat back as a plate of assorted appetizers was placed in the middle of the table. "Thanks, Roy," she said, smiling her best smile at the middle-aged man delivering the food.

He winked at her before turning back to weave through the tables to the kitchen.

Carrie had barely eaten her first onion ring when Kailey lifted her head, gave her curls a toss and called out, "Hey, Quinn! Why don't you and your friend come join us?"

Carrie kicked her under the table. She knew the toe of her boot had hit its mark when Kailey winced, then pasted on the same bright smile.

"I'm gonna get you for this," Carrie said as Quinn and Duke left their group and approached the table.

"Kailey." Quinn smiled down at her. "Planning on stirring up some sawdust on the dance floor tonight?"

"Maybe," she answered easily. Kailey and Quinn knew each other well. The two ranches backed on to each other and Kailey and Carrie had each taken turns babysitting Quinn's daughter, Amber, occasionally. He was a good-looking, hardworking man, but they'd known each other too long. They were colleagues hanging out, that was all.

Duggan, on the other hand, was familiar but very, very new. Looking at him resulted in a much different sensation than the one she got looking at Quinn. Something went all jumpy and swirly in her stomach, especially when he looked over at her with that same unsmiling expression. He'd removed his coat and hung it on one of the hooks along the back wall, and his blue-and-white striped shirt gave a clear indication of the breadth of his chest and flatness of his stomach. She wondered if he had a six-pack hiding under there.

"Help yourself," she offered, reaching for a jalapeño popper simply to keep her hands occupied. She took too big a bite, though, and the heat blasted her taste buds. To compensate, she reached for her glass and took a long gulp.

"Slow down, tiger." His voice came from close beside her, and she turned her head, a little too quickly it seemed. His eyes were too close, and while he still wasn't smiling, his eyes twinkled at her. Damned if he didn't make her feel about fifteen years old with that indulgent gleam in his eyes. Duke Duggan was a bit too big for his britches, in her mind.

"So you do remember how to speak to me," she said a little sharply. "I thought you'd forgotten this week."

The amused gaze faded a bit. "Forgotten?"

"It seemed every time I passed you and offered a hello, you were either focused on Quinn or simply ignored me."

He reached for a chicken wing. "Feelings hurt, Carrie?"

She didn't want to admit they had been. "Naw. I sort of expected city manners after all." She wasn't sure why she was antagonizing him. She really was glad he'd come home, and so was everyone at Crooked Valley. He was the answer to all the uncertainty they'd felt since Joe died. There was just something about him that set her on edge—in more ways than one.

One of the waitresses was passing by and Carrie inclined her chin. "Hey, Suze, a round on me, okay?"

Kailey was grinning widely now. "Just soda for me, Susan."

"I'll have a beer," Quinn said.

"Sweet tea," Duke ordered. "And the round's on *me*."

"Oh, I insist." Carrie smiled brightly. "Another rum and cola for me, please."

But Duke pulled out his wallet before Carrie could unzip her small purse. "I'm not in the habit of letting employees buy me drinks," he said quietly. Quinn and Kailey didn't hear, but Carrie did. The man sure did have a way of making a girl feel small.

"Employees," she replied tartly. "I guess Quinn and I know where we stand."

His brows pulled together. "That's not what I meant."

She shrugged. "Whatever." She reached for her chicken wing and didn't worry about being dainty as she ate it, wiping her saucy fingers on a paper napkin when she was done. Susan came back with their drinks and she let Duke pay. Why not, if he wanted to? She wasn't about to start a spitting match with him over a three-dollar beverage.

And just for spite, she picked up her drink and took a long, refreshing chug.

"So, Duke," Kailey said, dipping her onion ring in ketchup. "Are you really planning on staying on at the ranch?"

"I don't know," he replied, finally smiling. Carrie nearly dropped her second chicken wing. When he smiled, it was devastating. His whole face changed, his lips curved and his eyes crinkled at the corners while the rest of his facial muscles relaxed. When he wasn't brooding, he was incredibly attractive. And of course that smile had only blossomed on his face when Kailey addressed him. Jerk.

"Are you always going to go by that silly nickname?" Carrie asked, rolling her eyes a bit.

He raised an eyebrow. "I'm used to it. It's all I've been called since I was six years old." He turned away from her and smiled at Kailey. "When someone calls me Dustin, it makes me feel like my mom's calling me out for doing something wrong."

Carrie wiped her fingers and took another sip of her drink simply to hide her face. Duke suited him. Suited him better than Dustin. Dustin brought to mind a tall, gangly boy with thick, unruly hair and freckles. The man beside her was muscled, hard, 100 percent male, still with the hint of freckles under his tanned skin but with a no-nonsense military cut taming his cap of hair. More than that, it was his bearing. Solid and steady and a little bit dangerous. The kind of man you didn't want to cross, but the sort you felt completely safe with, too.

Well, mostly safe.

She looked up and caught him watching her and her heart did that weird thump thing again, feeling as if it was banging up against her rib cage while she grew hot all over.

Maybe Kailey was right. Maybe it had been too long

since she'd dated because she was definitely overre-
acting.

"So how'd you get the nickname anyway?" Quinn
asked, reaching for a jalapeño.

Duke grinned. "When I was six, we spent the summer here and my grandmother put all of us in summer
Bible school at the church. One day some kid was picking on my little sister. I cleaned his clock and told him
never to bother her again."

Everyone laughed a little, but Carrie wrinkled her
nose. "That still doesn't explain the name."

Duke met her gaze. "You know Joe. He loved his
John Wayne movies, and I sat through lots of show-
ings of *Rio Bravo*. When the kid apologized to Lacey,
I swaggered up to him, doing my best impression of the
Duke, and drawled, 'Sorry don't get it done, dude.' I've
been called Duke ever since."

Quinn and Kailey burst out laughing and even Carrie's lips tilted a little at the cute story. Duke's icy eyes
warmed a little as they fell upon her and his face relaxed. He wasn't the prettiest man she'd ever seen, but
there was something about him that was charismatic.
Sexy. Maybe it was his general aloofness blended with
moments of charm. Whatever it was, Carrie wasn't immune. Not even close.

A two-step that was popular on the radio these days
came on the speakers and Carrie's toe tapped along with
the opening bars. "Hey, Quinn," Kailey said loudly, to
be heard over the music. "You wanna take a turn on
the floor?"

Quinn smiled. "Why not?"

Carrie watched as Quinn and Kailey headed out to
the sawdust-covered floor and started circling the perimeter with the other dancers. Kailey was laughing

and Quinn was smiling. Carrie had once asked Kailey about why she didn't date Quinn—they got along great. Kailey confessed that once, before Quinn met his wife, they'd gone out on a couple of dates and that kissing him was like kissing a brother. There just wasn't any chemistry. Now that Quinn was a widower, they'd just stayed friends.

Carrie turned back to the table and her stomach flipped again. Duke was watching her, his gray-green eyes studying her as if he could see clear through her. She wasn't sure if she liked the sensation or if it made her uncomfortable. Before she could decide, he took a drink of his iced tea. "So," he said. "You and Kailey. She your wingman?"

Carrie nodded. "Yeah. Most of the time anyway. We've been friends a long time."

"She's a nice girl. I vaguely remember her from school."

"She's a bad influence," Carrie admitted. "And I love her for it. She keeps me from getting too boring."

"Are you boring, Carrie?"

She tried hard not to get lost in his eyes. "Occasionally. At least that's what I've been told."

He took a drink of his soda. "You weren't boring as a kid. Not as I recall anyway. I still remember the day in third grade when you put the frog in Jennifer Howard's lunch box."

Carrie couldn't stop the laugh that bubbled out of her mouth. "Oh, my gosh. I'd forgotten about that!"

"I'm sure Jennifer hasn't. She gave you the stink eye for months. I don't think I've ever heard quite that same combination of crying and grossing out since."

She took another drink of rum and realized she

needed to slow down. Carefully she put the glass back down on the table and stared at it for a few moments.

"So what changed?" Duke asked. "All work and no play? What turned that troublemaker into someone boring and responsible?"

Boring and responsible. When she'd looked at him talking to the other men earlier, those words had popped into her mind, too. Was it a case of pot meeting kettle?

She met his gaze and decided to be honest. It wasn't as though it was a big secret after all. "My mom got sick just before I graduated. Breast cancer."

"I'm sorry. Is she okay now?"

A lump formed in Carrie's throat. "No. She got through the first occurrence with surgery and chemo. It came back, though, more aggressive than before. She died two years ago."

"God." Duke put his hand over hers for a few seconds. It was warm and rough. "I didn't know. I wouldn't have brought it up..."

"It's okay." She tried to give him a reassuring smile, but she was sure it wobbled a bit around the edges. "It is what it is, right?"

"You and your dad must miss her so much." He slid his hand away.

And with that he scored another hit. Carrie absorbed the pain, knowing it was completely unintentional on his part. "My dad didn't take it so well. He turned to the bottle when she was doing her first round of chemo and barely hung on during her treatment. When she was rediagnosed, he fell apart. He left, and I haven't seen him since. In the end it was just Mom and me."

She didn't tell him to elicit his sympathy. She didn't want people to feel sorry for her. She gave her shoulders a shrug, loosening them up. "Anyway, I guess I put away childish things when that happened."

Yeah. Including disposable income. She'd gone from being a supportive daughter to assuming the mortgage for the house so the bank wouldn't foreclose when her father quit making the payments. Not to mention the medical bills and keeping the lights on. The few evenings she spent at the Dollar was about as exciting as her life got.

"I'm really sorry," he repeated. "How long have you been working at Crooked Valley?"

She smiled then, a genuine one, because she really did love her job. "Your grandfather hired me as a part-time hand when I was seventeen. I liked it so much I stayed on."

"And now you're my foreman. At thirty."

She shrugged, not particularly caring for the reminder of age. Kailey was twenty-eight and her mother was constantly asking when she was going to find a good man and settle down, that she wasn't getting any younger. It was as though a woman hit thirty and it was all on the downhill slide.

She peered into his face. "What about you, Duke? What keeps you from smiling more?"

He didn't answer, but he met her gaze and held it for a few long moments. "It's a long story."

She grinned. "It always is."

"Then, let's save it for another time." He treated her to a rare smile, small, but definitely friendly. "This is getting a bit heavy. Maybe we should hit the dance floor instead." He held out a hand.

Dance. With Duke. She blinked. The conversation had been serious, but the underlying attraction, at least on her part, was still there. Especially when he looked directly in her eyes like that.

"Um, okay." Her throat felt dry, so she grabbed her glass and finished what was left in the bottom, mentally promising herself to get a glass of water after this dance. Then she put her hand in his and stood up, her heart beating a little bit faster as they weaved their way to the floor with the other two-steppers.

Quinn and Kailey shuffled by, their boots stirring up sawdust as Duke put his hand on her waist and his other clasped her palm. Before she had a chance to take a deep breath, he started them moving around the floor with the other dancers. Carrie made herself relax and settle into the steps; she didn't want to trip over her own boots and look like an ass. Duke was a good dancer, smooth and even and confident, and with a change in pressure of his hand she knew to slide under and execute a smooth turn. When she was facing him again, he was smiling and the brilliant force of it nearly sucked the air from her lungs.

She was tipsy and dancing with her boss and thinking prurient thoughts about him. This was probably not the smartest thing to be doing on a Friday night.

They'd been late to the floor and the song ended not long after they'd begun dancing. They waited for the next, and Carrie was expecting something fast and fun. Instead the latest hot ballad boomed over the speakers and there was an awkward moment where they wondered whether to end the dance and go back to the table or carry through the next song.

"Care to?" His voice rumbled close to her ear again and she shivered.

"I guess," she answered, giving a little nod.

The dance hold was different this time, more intimate. His wide palm rode along the small of her back and his fingers curled around hers as he held her close. His belt buckle grazed the button of her jeans as they moved their feet, and her breasts pressed lightly against his shirtfront. Duke's shoulder was warm and hard beneath her fingertips—maybe he hadn't been ranching, but there was no denying that what was beneath the material was rock-solid.

The song went on and they moved along the floor like every other couple, but Carrie felt different. The air between them was taut with possibility; each place where their bodies touched was hypersensitive. Duke pulled her closer and his fingers kneaded against the small of her back, barely an inch above her tailbone. It would only take the slightest movement for her to have her head curled against his shoulder, to taste the skin of his neck. Instead she closed her eyes and took in the scent of him—warm skin and whatever aftershave he wore and something that was distinctly Duke without her being able to label it.

"What are we doing?" she whispered, but he didn't answer her. Instead his lips touched her temple, not quite a kiss but a deliberate contact—a caress—just the same.

Want spiraled through her. She wanted Duke Duggan. Wanted him to kiss her. Wanted to know what it felt like to have his hands on her. Wanted the rest of the people in the bar to disappear so they could have some privacy. This was crazy. She couldn't ever remember having this sort of instant reaction to a man. Maybe Kailey was right. Maybe it had been too long a dry spell.

The song went on and her body vibrated with anticipation and need. It was pointless, since in about one minute the song would end, they would part ways and she'd go back to the table and attempt to cool off. With water. Not with more rum. Maybe that was part of the problem....

The final chorus was waning when Duke leaned forward and whispered in her ear, "A few minutes after the song ends, I'm going to make my excuses and leave. I'll wait in my truck for ten minutes. If you want a drive home, I'll take you."

She snapped her head back and looked into his eyes. The fire that burned there made her weak in the knees. Was he saying what she thought he was saying? Could it be possible that he was feeling the same connection she was—and asking her to do something about it? "Are you sure? This is complicated...."

His gaze dropped to her lips and then back up to her eyes. "It doesn't have to be. Just two people cutting loose on a Friday night. Unless I misread the signals..."

She swallowed and shook her head quickly. "No... you didn't. But..."

"I'm not in the market for a girlfriend," he assured her, his hand squeezing at her hip. "Knowing that, if you want a drive home, meet me in the parking lot."

The song ended. Duke stepped back and raised a finger to his hat. "Thanks for the dance, Carrie."

She had to be out of her mind to even consider taking him up on his offer. Duke walked away, heading straight to the bar where he clapped Quinn on the back and ordered up another drink, looking entirely calm while her whole body was on high alert.

Carrie weaved her way back to the table where Kailey was waiting, virtually bouncing in her chair.

"Oh, my God. You and Duke were smokin' out there! What the heck?"

"We just danced," Carrie insisted, though she was

still so keyed up she felt as if she might bust out of her skin.

"Just danced my eye. It was like electricity between you. Wow."

"Shut up, Kailey." Carrie didn't know what to do. She was tempted, oh, so tempted by Duke's unexpected offer. She was a thirty-year-old woman and her sex life was nonexistent. Here was a man, a gorgeous man, propositioning her for...for what? A night of mind-blowing sex? He'd made it clear he didn't want a relationship. She wished she could be more blasé. She knew these things happened all the time. But they didn't happen to *her*. Could she really do it?

It all sounded absolutely perfect except for two nagging thoughts. One, he was her boss. And two, she'd learned a long, long time ago that even the best-sounding ideas came with consequences. It was the consequences she tried to avoid.

A waitress stopped by the table and put down fresh drinks. "From the gentleman at the bar," she said with a smile.

Carrie looked up. Duke met her gaze evenly and saluted her with his glass, then proceeded to drain his drink and, true to his word, headed for the door.

"What was all that about?" Kailey asked, sipping her soda through a pink straw.

Carrie looked down so Kailey couldn't see the heat in her cheeks. "Nothing. He just bought us drinks."

She couldn't do this, she decided. She'd be crazy. Never in her life had she hooked up for anything casual. It just wasn't her style. And yet there was something exciting about it, too, something risky and dangerous. Maybe she should stop being so uptight. Maybe a night with Duke was just what she needed to unwind a little bit and chill out?

"And he just walked out the door. Without Quinn."

Carrie looked up and wasn't surprised to see Kailey's eyebrow quirked knowingly. She wasn't fooling her friend a bit. "So I, uh, might have another drive home," she said, the nerves twisting around in her stomach again.

"Oh. My. God." Kailey repeated and leaned forward. "He's waiting for you, isn't he?"

"Shh. Not so loud!" Carrie hissed urgently. "I don't need it broadcast through the bar, you know!"

"Shut up! You're going to do it? You're going to go home with him?" Her eyes lit up. "You go, girl! It's about time!"

"I don't know," Carrie said miserably. "I mean, he wasn't exactly the epitome of friendliness the other day. And then we started talking and dancing and…" She met Kailey's gaze. "There's definitely something. But he's my boss. It would probably be a huge mistake."

"Sweetie, you could stand to make a mistake now and again."

"I know. I'm dull."

"You're careful, and I get why." Kailey put a hand on Carrie's arm. "Look, I think he's a stand-up guy and so does Quinn. Go. If you change your mind, it's no big deal. One of us should find out if he's a good kisser, and he didn't look twice at me. If he's dynamite, I can be jealous later."

"What if he…we…"

Kailey's blue eyes met Carrie's, serious now. "Then you take precautions." Kailey picked up her purse, rooted around for a moment, and then she slipped her hand across the table and tucked something into Carrie's palm. Carrie knew from the rough edge of the square packet that it was a condom.

For the first time, Carrie wished she was as sexually confident as her friend. She didn't know how to do this.

"How long is he waiting?" Kailey asked.

Carrie checked her watch. "Another few minutes." She looked at Kailey. "You'll be okay?"

"Of course. Don't worry about me. I'll probably give Quinn a lift home anyway. Go."

Before she could change her mind, Carrie got to her feet and chugged back the last of her liquid courage. Then she grabbed her purse, took a big breath and smiled at Kailey. "Wish me luck," she said, and she saw Kailey's lips form the words *good luck* but didn't hear her over the new song that started up.

Anxiety and excitement threaded through her veins as she wound her way through the bar to the door and stepped outside into the cold air. Maybe he'd gone already...

But there he was, leaning against the fender of his pickup truck, his arms crossed over his chest and his cowboy hat shadowing his eyes.

Then he saw her and he smiled, uncrossing his arms and pushing away from the truck. Carrie's feet took her one step forward, then another, and another...until she was at the truck and he was holding the door open for her.

Chapter Three

She'd actually come.

Duke hadn't expected her to. Carrie struck him as the buttoned-down type that maybe got out now and again with her girlfriends to cut loose but wasn't out on the prowl. She was too sweet. Too reserved. Her friend Kailey was more on the vivacious side and good for a laugh. But it wasn't Kailey he'd danced with. It wasn't Kailey who'd captured his attention.

It was Carrie, and her sun-streaked hair, big eyes and sad smile. His response to her had been instant and exciting, and before he could think better of it he'd made his proposition. Once outside, though, the cold air had brought him to his senses. He was ten kinds of fool. She wasn't some girl hanging around a bar on base, looking for a good time. She was Carrie Coulter. Freckle Face. His employee, for God's sake. What a dumb idea.

He looked over at her as he turned on the heater and put the truck in Reverse. The way her jaw was tensed, she was as nervous as he was. He'd waited for her because he'd said he would, but he hadn't truly thought she'd take him up on his offer. He'd never actually made that sort of proposition before, and he'd figured he'd blown it. Watching her come out the doors and into the parking lot had set his heart racing. His confidence had taken quite a beating lately, but maybe he had more going for him than he realized.

Either that or Carrie Coulter was desperate.

He couldn't help but chuckle at the thought. More desperate than he was? Not likely. What a pair they made. Secretly, he was glad to be out of the bar. The noise had been overwhelming and instead of relaxing, he'd found himself tensing up. Just trying to hear the conversations going on around him took all his focus. Now he was sitting here, away from the crowd, and neither of them was saying anything.

"What's so funny?" she asked, turning her head to look at him, chafing her hands together.

"Nothing," he answered, but judging by the look on her face, she didn't believe him. "I really didn't think you'd come."

"I had second thoughts. And third and fourth."

Intrigued, he checked the road and then glanced back at her again. "But you came anyway."

"Let's not analyze it to death," she suggested, and he chuckled again. Dammit, he enjoyed her. He liked how she shot straight from the hip without trying to impress, liked the way she smiled and really liked the way she smelled when she was snuggled close in his arms—like shampoo and fresh air and some sort of light perfume, all of it magnified by the heat of her body against his.

It was one thing to proposition a woman on the dance floor and another to wait and then spend fifteen minutes in a vehicle, prolonging things to close to half an hour. It gave a person way too much time to think, and so it was that as Duke turned down the side road leading to Carrie's house, he felt compelled to let her off the hook.

"We don't have to do this, you know."

Her head snapped to the left and he felt her gaze burn into the side of his head. "You don't want to?"

Damn. "It's not that. It's just...I don't want you to feel pressured if you've changed your mind." His fingers tightened on the wheel. Why the heck was he so nervous all of a sudden? *Nervous* wasn't generally part of his vocabulary. He normally made a decision and got on with it, no second thoughts, no reservations.

Until two months ago. Until the IED had changed everything. He'd gone from being 100 percent sure of himself to questioning every single decision. He didn't even know why he felt like such a failure. The explosion hadn't been his fault. He'd merely been in the wrong place at the wrong time.

She didn't say anything, so he let out a breath and said, "You'll have to tell me which mailbox is yours."

A few hundred yards more and Carrie pointed with her finger. "The next one," she said quietly, and he slowed, his headlights sweeping a swath of light across her front lawn as he pulled into her driveway. Her truck sat beneath the protection of a carport next to the bungalow, a model only slightly newer than his with rust spots around the license plate.

He pulled to a stop, killed the engine, and silence settled around them in the twilight.

He wasn't sure how to start. Wasn't that the darndest thing?

"So, uh...thanks for the drive," Carrie said, and without looking at him, she put her hand on the door handle and pulled.

Panic shot through his veins and he reached out, grabbing the wrist of her left hand before she could get out of the vehicle. "Don't go," he said roughly, wondering how he could have messed things up so completely

Several seconds spun out while Duke tried to regain his equilibrium and common sense. "Whew," he finally said, down low. "Okay. Okay."

"You're not mad?"

"Of course not." He frowned. "You always have the right to say no, you know."

"I thought you'd be disappointed."

And, oh, he was. His body was still jacked up from all the stimulation, and he was going to have to find some sort of displacement activity to burn off the energy. "Hell yeah," he murmured, running his finger over her bare shoulder. "I'd be lying if I said I wasn't. But not disappointed in you. Right now I'm just cursing your sensible side. You've got me wound pretty tight, Miss Coulter."

"It would appear we have some chemistry going on."

He chuckled. "And that's the understatement of the century."

He bent and picked up her top and helped her get it over her head, but she wore it without her bra, and the idea of her bare breasts beneath the fabric didn't help deflate his libido one bit. As he shrugged on his own shirt, she hiccuped softly and he knew without a doubt that she'd been right to put on the brakes. She wasn't drunk but she wasn't quite sober either, and he didn't want that on his conscience. If they ever did go through with it, he wanted her clearheaded and present for every single second....

And that line of thinking wasn't helping cool his jets, either.

"I should go," he said quietly. "Are you going to be okay?"

She made a dismissive sound. "I'm not that drunk."

He laughed. "No, ma'am." He went forward and put

a finger beneath her chin, lifted it and dropped a light kiss on her lips. "You are, however, a very difficult woman to walk away from."

He'd surprised her with that. He could tell in the way her lips dropped open the slightest bit and her eyes widened.

"It's probably better this way anyway," she said, stepping back. "If we…you know…it would be awkward at the ranch."

Only if they let it be, but he understood her concern. "I had a nice time tonight," he admitted. "And that was unexpected, so thank you, Carrie."

She nodded quickly. "Me, too."

"I'll be going, then. Unless…"

There was a short pause. "No, it's better this way. I'll see you later."

It was another awkward moment where neither of them seemed sure what the right next move was, so Duke stepped forward and placed a kiss on her forehead before sliding out the door and heading for his truck.

He was backing out of her driveway when a light came on inside, and when he went to put the truck in Drive he noticed his hands were shaking.

It bothered him to realize how much he'd truly wanted to stay. And bothered him even more to know that he'd temporarily lost his mind simply because he'd danced with her. Who knew a woman could have such a rapid and visceral effect on him?

It was going to be a problem, though he would never admit that to Carrie. He'd have to either forget about her or get her out of his system. Considering she would be at the ranch day in and day out, forgetting didn't seem like the most likely option.

CARRIE'S HEAD SEEMED to pulse at the same tempo as her heartbeat. She swiped her hand across her eyes, scraping away the grittiness in the corners and wincing at the pain that throbbed just behind her forehead.

Stupid rum and cola.

Sun glinted through the blinds she'd forgotten to shut last night, and she squinted. What time was it? A quick check of her ancient clock radio said eight forty-five. She couldn't remember the last time she'd slept this late. As she sat up in bed, the room took an uncertain shift. She waited it out, then cautiously stood, shut her blinds, and went in search of acetaminophen and a large glass of water in an attempt to rehydrate.

It was half-gone when there was a knock on her door.

Probably Kailey, Carrie mused, shuffling her way to the foyer. She'd want a play-by-play of last night for sure. Instead she opened the door to find Duke on the step holding a cardboard tray with two coffees and a smile.

She then realized that she was in her panties and the same red shirt—still minus her bra—that she'd been wearing when she fell into bed after he left. His smile was replaced by a slightly shocked expression that mellowed to amusement. "I'd offer you hair of the dog," he said warmly, "except I thought you'd appreciate coffee more."

She would not freak out that he was seeing her in her underwear. She would not. "Gimme," she muttered instead, and reached for the tray. As she disappeared into the kitchen, she called back, "You coming in or what?"

She heard his boots hit the tile and the door shut behind him. "How could I refuse such a warm invitation?" he responded, coming through to her small kitchen. He looked her up and down. "Do you always answer your door in your underwear?"

"I thought you were Kailey."

"Right." He grinned at her. She really wished he'd stay grouchy and broody. He was easier to dislike then.

"You didn't need to bring coffee over."

"I thought you might be a little worse for wear this morning, that's all."

Which she was. Not that she'd had trouble sleeping. But she distinctly remembered dreams last night. Dreams about Duke and what might have happened in his truck. Or inside. She wondered if the reality was even half as good as her dreams, and if it was, she discovered she quite regretted putting a halt to their activities.

Sort of. Because her body was sorry but her brain was a bit blown away by the sheer force of their chemistry. It was too much. Overwhelming. The kind of thing that could swallow a girl up and then spit her out.

"Give me a minute to pull on some pants, okay?" Avoiding his assessing gaze, she resisted the urge to scoot to her bedroom for proper clothing, instead taking calm, measured steps. It wasn't as if she was naked....

Which she very well might have been if they'd finished what they started and were dealing with a true morning after.

She returned to the kitchen feeling seminormal, dressed in jeans and a hooded sweatshirt and her hair scraped back into a ponytail. The coffee smelled delicious, so she reached for her cup and took a cautious sip while Duke watched her over the rim of his own, his hips resting against the kitchen counter and his left foot crossed over his right. He looked ultrarelaxed when she was anything but.

Maybe walking away hadn't messed with his sleep the way it had hers.

"Thanks for this," she said, cupping her hands around the heat sleeve. "But you really didn't need to come by. I'm fine."

"Actually, I wanted to apologize."

"You did?" She raised an eyebrow at him. "What on earth for?"

He looked oddly embarrassed as his gaze dropped to the floor for a moment and his cheeks grew ruddy. He looked up and gave a small, slightly crooked smile. "Look, Freckles, it's pretty clear that we've got chemistry. But I shouldn't have let it get in the way of my common sense. You were right last night about it being an awkward situation."

Chemistry, hah. Carrie remembered the old trick from high school where a bunch of them had dropped a Mentos into a bottle of cola. That was chemistry, too, and that was just about how she'd felt last night. Fizzy. Explosive.

And why on earth did she feel all girlie when he called her Freckles?

"What, you've shortened Freckle Face to just Freckles?" She ignored the other stuff he'd said—she didn't feel like going into a postmortem of "let's define our relationship parameters" while her head was still throbbing.

"Too many syllables." Duke's lips twitched and he took another long drink of his coffee.

"Don't worry about last night. It's already forgotten." Yeah, and her nose was about to grow *à la* Pinocchio. As if she'd ever forget straddling him in his truck or the way he'd carried her inside as if it was his single purpose in life.

"Deal," he agreed.

Now that it was settled, Duke seemed to relax and look around him. "So. This was the house you grew up in, huh."

She nodded, knowing how it must appear to Duke. The house was nothing special. Things had fallen into a bit of disrepair, though Carrie did her best as a handyman. Maintenance usually took up what little budget she had for household items, so she hadn't really had a chance to put her own personal stamp on the place in the form of homey, decorative touches. Not that decorating was really on her list of strengths...

"I love it here. When Mom got sick again and my dad took off, I talked the bank into letting me assume the mortgage."

"As a ranch hand? You weren't foreman then, were you? Wow. I'm impressed they lent you the money."

She shook her head. "I know you and your grandfather weren't close, but he was really good to me. He cosigned the loan. It was the only way they'd approve me."

"That was good of him."

He sounded sincere, and she was glad. "So much had changed in my life. I think it was a relief to have this house, some sort of consistency. Plus it let Mom stay here during most of her illness."

"That must have been hard." He watched her over the rim of his cup, his gaze steady on her face. One thing she'd say about Duke, when you spoke to him, he paid attention.

She met his gaze. "Yeah, it was," she said quietly. Harder still had been the last days, when she'd had to give in to harsh reality and her mom had gone to a hospice in Great Falls. It had meant that Carrie couldn't be with her as much as she wanted. It had meant that she'd missed her opportunity to say a last goodbye, too. That was something she'd always regret.

"It must have been tough, being the main bread-winner."

She shrugged. "You do what you have to do. All I can say is I'm glad the ranch is still running. Without this job, I'd lose the house, and I'm still paying off the medical bills."

She met Duke's gaze and saw the expected sympathy. "Hey, don't feel sorry for me," she said. "I'm still healthy as a horse. It's all good. What about you? How're you settling in at Crooked Valley?"

It was Duke's turn to make a face. "Honestly? That house is too big and quiet for me. Quinn's got his office in the downstairs, and I felt like a fool wandering through it all alone. I moved my things into the bunk-house."

Carrie put her coffee cup in the trash. "The bunk-house is all right. Quinn never used it because he has the house nearby and he's got Amber, too. But it had to be in rough shape. No one's lived in it for quite a while."

Duke nodded. "It needed some work. I spent a few days last week cleaning it from top to bottom and dropping some money at the hardware store. I've been doing odd jobs in between shadowing Quinn around and getting an overall feeling for the operation. There's more here than I remember."

"Your grandfather added the bucking stock in the past ten years. It didn't take off the way he hoped. He needs a Kailey."

"A Kailey?"

"She runs the program at Brandt. Our stock has potential, but needs dedicated attention. And that's not my specialty. Nor Quinn's. He does the best he can, but he's not a rodeo guy."

Duke started to laugh. "You know who'd be good at that? My brother, Rylan."

"I heard a rumor he was still competing." Rylan, three years younger than Duke, who'd moved to the city and then surprised everyone by becoming a bareback rider. "Joe wanted him to come back, too, you know. He always refused."

Duke nodded, then finished his coffee and threw his cup in her garbage can. "I know. Ry was determined to make it his own way. He's more stubborn than I am."

"God forbid," she said drily, and Duke's eyes twinkled at her.

"Ry doesn't want handouts. I get that. He got one of these letters, too—that is, if he stayed in one place long enough for the lawyers to find him."

"He did?"

Duke nodded. "You didn't read the whole thing, did you? The ranch is left to all three of us. I only own a third."

Of course. She'd been silly to think that Joe would have left everything to Duke. "So he's coming back?"

Duke's face clouded over. "I don't know. We haven't spoken."

"But he's your brother." Growing up, Carrie would have given her left arm for a sibling. Someone to talk to and hang out with and share clothes with—who wasn't a friend from school. Someone to share memories of her parents with or turn to with secrets and support. "Surely you guys speak to each other."

"Not so much."

"And you and Lacey?"

Duke frowned. "I saw her when I was first back.

She's been through a divorce, and she's working for Natural Resources and Conservation."

Carrie looked up at him. "You've got a family and you don't even seem to care. Trust me when I say they might not always be there."

"I know that. I lost my father, remember?"

"So what's keeping you from the rest of your family?"

He pushed away from the counter. "I just came to bring you coffee. I should probably be going."

"I hit a nerve," she acknowledged. "What are you hiding, Duke?"

"I'm not hiding anything. I'm back, I was at loose ends, I got the summons. I'm just here until I can figure out what I want to do next."

A cold sensation ran down Carrie's body. "What do you mean, you're just here until…? What happens to the ranch if you leave?"

He shrugged. "We all have to take our place at some point during the year. If we don't, the ranch gets sold."

Sold out from under them all, and if things went the way they had been lately, the buyer would sell off the herd and turn the ranch land into a housing development. She'd be out of a job. Instead of Duke being some savior, it was a real possibility that this was just prolonging the inevitable. Maybe she should start looking for new employment now, so she didn't end up scrambling. Didn't end up defaulting on loans and payments.

The problem was she loved Crooked Valley. It was her home. A home Duke didn't appreciate at all.

"I see," she said weakly. "So why bother learning the ropes if you're just going to pick up and move on again?"

"What if I don't pick up and move? As I said, I'm

figuring out what to do next. Learning about the operation is interesting."

Carrie's hopes were short-lived. Ranchers didn't find things "interesting." Ranching was part of who they were. It was something that was in the blood. It definitely wasn't something to dabble in for fun or because you had nothing better to do. Duke would stay a few months and be gone.

"Crooked Valley isn't really the sort of place where you just fill some of your spare time," she replied, her voice sharp. The headache was threatening to come back, too.

"Hey, give me a break. I haven't come anywhere close to making any sort of a decision. I've only been here a week. I've hardly had two seconds to wrap my head around all of this, let alone relax."

"Well," she replied, "you'd better brace yourself, then, because next weekend things are going to get a lot busier and we need every pair of hands available."

"Get ready for what?"

"You want a taste of what ranching is really like? We move the herd back here to the mountain pastures for the winter. The folks at the Triple B will give us a hand driving the cattle, and the next week we return the favor. It's exhausting but huge fun, too."

"A cattle drive?"

She nodded. "Yup. We overnight at the old cookhouse and ride back the next day. When your grandmother was still alive, she cooked for two straight days to feed the crew when they returned. The past few years Joe brought in sandwiches and coffee for the first night's supper and we did a potluck on the return. All the wives bring dishes and someone generally fires up some music for a bit of dancing." She knew there was a hint of nostalgia in her voice but she couldn't help it. It was one of the hardest and best weekends of the year, in her opinion—second only to the branding and vaccination day in the spring.

"I'm expected to coordinate that?" Duke's eyebrows lifted. "Why didn't anyone mention it?"

She shrugged. "I thought Quinn would have told you. Until last night, you barely said two words to me all week."

Duke shoved his hands in his pockets. "I have no idea what I'm doing when it comes to herding cows. And I have no idea what to do about after, either. Do people expect a party?" He looked genuinely distressed. "You'll help me, right?"

Ah, so here it was. Now that he was stuck he realized she existed. *That's not fair,* a voice inside her argued. *He sure knew you existed last night.*

Yeah. He knew she existed when it came to making out in his truck or needing a social coordinator. She lifted her chin. "Forget it, Duke. I'm the cattle foreman and I'll be heading up the drive. I'm not a party planner."

Chapter Four

For a girl who was looking a bit worse for wear after her night on the town, she sure wasn't giving an inch. He already felt out of his depth, and now he was expected to host some sort of social event at the ranch? It didn't help that Carrie was being stubborn and he had to sweeten her up somehow. It was his first real test at Crooked Valley and he didn't want to blow it.

"Of course I don't expect you to plan it," he replied, trying to smile at her. "Maybe you could just tell me what I need to do. Make me a list or something."

"A list? Really?"

"Sure, why not?" He raised an eyebrow. "Rather than stand in your kitchen, which is charming by the way, why don't I take you out for breakfast?" He leaned in conspiratorially. "I usually find the best thing for a hangover is orange juice, bacon and eggs cooked in the bacon grease. The diner still serves that stuff, right?"

She looked tempted. It was a good sign.

"Come on, Freckles. You don't have to go to work. Let me treat you to breakfast and you can tell me all the stuff I need to do before this big weekend coming up."

"I need to clean my house...."

"How dirty can it be?" he argued. "You're the only

one here to mess it up. It's just breakfast," he challenged her. "Not a proposal of marriage."

"You're aggravating."

But her voice had softened and he could tell she was wavering. He grinned. "So I've been told."

"You're buying?"

"Of course. It's the least I can do in exchange for your help." But her question really did make him think. How hard were things for Carrie? Other than her night at the bar, there was nothing in her life to make him think she was extravagant with her money. The house was plain and her truck was old. And a night out with a friend did not constitute extravagance. Everyone deserved to get out once in a while.

"I guess I could. I am kind of hungry."

Score. He nodded at her. "Great. You might want to just wash your face before we go."

Her lips dropped open and her eyes registered dismay. "My face? What's wrong with my face?"

He slid his index finger under his eye. "You melted a bit during the night."

She spun on her heel and disappeared into the bathroom. Two seconds later a squeal erupted, echoing off the bathroom tile. "I look like a raccoon! Why didn't you tell me?"

"I thought I just did." He walked down the hall and glanced in the bathroom. She ran a cloth beneath a stream of water, wrung it out and scrubbed at her eyes.

"This is why I don't wear eyeliner," she groused. "Or much makeup at all. I never remember to wash my face before bed and then I get up looking like..." She broke off the sentence. "Well. Looking like this."

What he thought was that she didn't need makeup to be beautiful, but he wouldn't say that because after last night it would take on importance that he didn't want. Or maybe he did want it but he shouldn't, which came out to practically the same thing. Mouth closed. Boundaries set.

"Okay. I think I'm okay now. Oh, wait. I need to brush my teeth. They're fuzzy."

He chuckled. "The rum really got to you, huh."

She avoided his gaze. "I'd actually prefer not to talk about last night."

"Fine by me." Talking about it would create one of two outcomes. Either they'd argue or they'd pick up where they left off. He didn't want the first and he was telling himself he'd better not indulge in the second. Last night he'd been carried away. It had been nice talking to someone. To hold her close, to feel so alive. Truth was, since his accident he hadn't felt that kind of vitality. In the end it wouldn't be smart carrying on with her, though. She worked for him, and he definitely couldn't afford for her to quit.

He waited while she brushed her teeth and spit in the sink, and then they left the house together. When she suggested taking her own truck so she could pick up some groceries after, he didn't argue. He was quickly learning Carrie was independent and used to making her own decisions—and getting her way.

Duke backed out of the driveway first and headed toward town. The Horseshoe Diner was on the main drag, sporting a scarred asphalt parking lot and a neon horseshoe sign with about three bulbs burned out on one side. Duke pulled in and parked and then waited for Carrie. She parked beside him and hopped out, looking a little better since driving with the window down a bit. She might be hungover but she was definitely stubborn.

Once inside they found a table near the window and

a waitress he didn't recognize brought over menus and filled their coffee cups. He opened his plastic-covered menu and scanned the breakfast items, but Carrie left hers closed. Yeah, he'd been away from Gibson for a long time. Probably too long. Carrie knew the menu by heart and he felt like a complete stranger.

The damnedest thing was that he'd stayed away to prove a point. To prove he was Evan Duggan's kid, to prove he wanted to follow in his dad's footsteps and not be pushed into Joe Duggan's dreams for his son.

But he was coming to realize that by doing that, he'd also turned his back on something really important. This was where his father had grown up. Gone to school. Had his hopes and dreams. But despite the honor of serving his country, it had always been clear that Evan had disappointed the family. It didn't matter that Joe was gone. Duke was the one here now and he was afraid that he'd continue that legacy, too. And if he failed at this, too, he was left with nothing.

"You got awfully quiet." Carrie's voice interrupted his thoughts and he was grateful for the distraction.

"Just deciding what to get. It all looks good. And huge." He turned his attention back to the menu and its country-size offerings.

When the waitress came back, Duke ordered pancakes and sausages while Carrie asked for the Cowboy's Breakfast. A quick scan showed that it was a hearty meal—bacon, sausage and ham, two eggs, toast and home fries. "You're going to eat all that?" he asked when the waitress was gone, and she nodded.

"Breakfast is the most important meal of the day." She sipped at the orange juice that had been delivered and licked her lips. "Besides, people in glass houses shouldn't throw stones. You haven't seen the size of Rosie's pancakes. They're like hubcaps."

He was hungry, so the idea of huge pancakes sounded awesome. "I think I'll manage. Maybe I'll take some home with me for later. And speaking of, how much food am I going to need next weekend anyway? How does that work, with the night at the cookhouse? Who takes the food and stuff?"

Carrie looked up at him and felt her heart soften even though she didn't want it to. He was trying, bless him, and she'd been a little short with him back at the house but it was only because over the years she'd taken her share of crap from the men in the area. Not everyone had been as open-minded as Joe about letting her supervise the entire cattle operation. It wasn't just about grazing the cattle and making sure they had food and water before being sold. It was about producing the best beef possible and getting the best price possible. There was a science to it she enjoyed, even if at times it made her head hurt with all the complexities.

She'd had to learn on the job and so did Duke, so maybe she should give him a break.

"Usually a few people go up the day before. We use the quads for that, and take up food, supplies, make sure the cots are set out and things are cleaned up." She grinned. "It's outhouse facilities, though we do have propane and running water in the cookhouse. That's a lot faster than trying to do that the day of the drive."

"You still do this stuff from horseback?"

She nodded. "Yeah. And we try not to use the quads that much anyway. Horses are gentler on the environment." She smiled at him. "How long has it been since you were on horseback, Duke?"

Their food was delivered so he didn't answer for a

minute, but once they were alone again he reached for the syrup and admitted, "A long time."

She chuckled as she put a splotch of ketchup on her plate. "You might want to get in the saddle right away, then. Or you'll be regretting it after a day and a half of riding."

"You're right." He looked down at his plate. "You were right about the pancakes, too. Hubcaps. But delicious hubcaps."

Between the coffee and juice, Carrie was feeling better, but she took a bite of fried egg and closed her eyes with gratitude. Duke was right. Eggs fried in bacon grease were awesome after a night of indulgence. She nearly felt human. And hungry.

For the next several minutes they talked about the drive and the supplies that Duke would need. Now that the initial shock was over, he seemed keen for the event. So much so that when she suggested he maybe sit the ride out and look after the other details, he shook his head and flat-out refused.

"I want to learn these sorts of things. I don't want to slow you down, but I'd like to carry my weight."

She had to respect him for that, and he earned bonus points for realizing that there was a learning curve to driving cattle. "I can give you some pointers," she suggested, dipping a fried potato in her ketchup. "And on the day I'll pair you up with someone so you can work together."

"Thanks, Carrie." Duke mopped up some pancake in a pool of syrup. "Do I need to be in touch with anyone about the potluck?"

She grinned. He really was a newbie, wasn't he? "No," she laughed. "When we get back, everyone will take an hour to clean up at home, and then come back with the food and ready to enjoy themselves. All you have to do is provide the space." Full, she pushed her plate a little to the side. "That's how we roll around here, Duggan. It's a community. The following weekend we'll help out the Triple B and they'll do the same thing, only their drive is shorter and there's no overnight. We just have to hope there's no heavy snow between now and then. Hopefully it'll hold off until Thanksgiving."

She knew that was a big hope; snow in November was the norm around here. At least the Duggan grazing land was far enough south that it rarely got too deep. Then in the spring, they'd move the herd back down to the river pastures.

"You doing anything for the holiday?" he asked, cutting into a perfectly browned breakfast sausage.

Grief cut into Carrie. Since her mom died, Joe had been the closest thing she had to family. She and Quinn and Amber had always been invited up to the big house for holiday celebrations so that none of them had to face spending them alone. Everyone contributed to the food and they'd shared lots of laughs, though Carrie had known each time that Joe was missing his family.

"Did I say something wrong?" Duke's gaze was fixed on her face, concern etched in his features. "Here." He handed over a napkin.

She hadn't even realized that a few tears had slid from the corners of her eyes. "Sorry," she apologized, dabbing at the tears. "I got a little sentimental. The past few years Joe invited Quinn and me to the house. I was just realizing that he isn't going to be here this year."

"You miss him."

"Of course I do. He was the closest thing to family I had left." She gave him a stern stare. "For you guys, too, you know. It wouldn't have killed you to visit more often."

"I know," Duke said quietly.

"Why didn't you?" She didn't understand. Joe Duggan had been strong, kind, generous. Maybe the ranch hadn't been the biggest or the best in the state but he'd been proud of it just the same. Proud of his son, too. Though she doubted if Duke would appreciate her saying anything to that effect.

As if he'd suddenly lost his appetite, Duke set his plate aside. "Because I knew what he'd want. He'd want me to accept the life that my dad never did. My father gave his life for his country but that wasn't good enough. He was supposed to dedicate his life to Crooked Valley, and my grandfather never got over the fact that Dad's choice was not the same as his. I'm the eldest. I know what Joe wanted. He wanted me to live the life that was meant for my father. And I wanted to make my own choice."

"Maybe," she said softly, "he just wanted his legacy to live on somehow. Out here farms are a family business. But Joe and Eileen didn't have a big family. Evan was it. Joe worked so hard to make something of this place and no one was interested."

Duke's eyes appeared troubled. "You think I don't know that? But it's different when…"

"When what?" she asked quietly. "When you're carrying the expectations of a family on your shoulders?"

"Something like that," he admitted.

"Duke, in theory we should all be able to make our own choices. But sometimes life makes choices for us and it turns out to be the best thing in the end."

His gaze locked with hers. "And how have those life choices worked out for you so far, Carrie?"

The question stung because she knew what he saw when he looked at her. Small-town girl stuck in the same small town, parents gone, spending her days chasing cattle around. It also made her sad because he didn't understand that there was nothing better than riding out on a clear summer morning with the scent of fresh hay and wildflowers in the air, or the pure satisfaction of physical exhaustion at the end of the day. Sunsets over the creek, a fresh blanket of snow and the smell of evergreens in the forest.

He felt sorry for her. And she felt sorry for him.

"Maybe one day you'll understand." She picked up her purse. "I should get going. I have errands to run before going home. Thanks for breakfast."

She got up from the table and made to leave, but he reached out and grabbed her wrist. "Hey. I didn't mean to make you mad."

She looked down at him, emotions swirling. She was a little annoyed with him, felt a little pity, too, and then there was this thing between them that reared up every time they touched. Right now his fingers seemed to burn through the skin at her wrist, and her mind raced back to only twelve hours earlier when they'd been nearly naked in her kitchen.

Crazy. That was what she was.

"I'm not mad." Her voice was low so she wouldn't be overheard. "You just need to realize that what I do doesn't feel like a punishment to me. Not like it does to you. What do you think you're being punished for anyway?"

And there was the confusion in his eyes again, the troubled expression that made her want to curl up in his arms and see if he needed to talk it out. It was the oddest sensation. She'd never considered herself a nurturer before. She was far more comfortable dealing with livestock than people's emotions.

He let go of her wrist. "You'd better get to those errands," he said. "I'll see you Monday."

And that was it. Whatever attraction was between them needed to be ignored, and she had to focus on her job. There was a lot to do before next weekend's drive and she couldn't let herself get distracted.

With her purse over her shoulder, she left the diner and stepped out into the sunshine.

Chapter Five

Duke shifted the reins in his hands and followed the line of horses through the gully toward the smattering of buildings that made up the river base of the ranch. Along with Quinn, Carrie and three ranch hands, they were joined by four men from the Triple B. Ten altogether and Carrie the only woman in the bunch. She rode ahead, talking to Quinn, and Duke couldn't help but admire her figure on horseback. She'd barely said two words to him this morning, though, other than asking him if he was ready. Since breakfast the previous weekend, they'd kept their conversations strictly businesslike.

That hadn't stopped him from admiring the view of her in a pair of worn jeans, or the way her ponytail curled over her collar, or the bright blue of her eyes, which seemed even bluer in the clear, cold air.

Today she was bundled up in a puffy jacket, knitted hat and thick leather gloves, protection against the cold. It had snowed overnight and the horses made tracks through two inches of fresh snow. Duke found himself glad they weren't doing this later in the season. If the weather held, tomorrow was going to be chilly but clear.

They came up out of the gully and there it was—a small bunkhouse, probably not more than four or five hundred square feet, a shed, a longer, rectangular building that Duke figured was the cookhouse and a rough-looking but sturdy shelter that fronted a fenced corral.

It looked abandoned.

Chatter got louder as they entered the yard in front of the biggest building. Carrie circled around and came to the back, trotting up beside him, a big smile on her face. "This is it," she called out. "What do you think?"

He wasn't sure what to think. Twenty years ago these buildings hadn't even been on the property. They looked to be in decent shape, but they looked lonely, too.

"I don't remember this. I didn't realize the ranch had grown so much."

"We're not a huge operation, but we hold our own, and having the river base makes sense. It gets more use in the summertime. Not the cookhouse, so much. But the bunkhouse. It's a bit on the small side, but if we have to be down here for some reason, it gives us a warm and dry place to stay."

She smiled at him, the first real smile he'd gotten out of her since last week's parting. "The river's not far, and the fishing's good. It was built for ranch business, but it makes a good getaway for a few days, too."

"Do you ever need to get away?" he asked. "Seems to me with all this wide-open space, a getaway might involve something a little more refined than fishing and sleeping on a saggy cot."

"Don't knock it until you try it," she suggested, and dismounted. "Hey, Jack," she called out. "If you'll look after Sage for me, I'll get the place unlocked and the heater started up." She reached into her pocket and took out a key.

"It's locked?" Duke hopped down from his mount—

a black gelding named Badger—and clutched the reins in his hand as he followed her.

She shrugged as she took a single step onto a porch and fit the key into the lock. "It keeps the honest people out. You never know who might end up out here."

"What if someone got stranded or lost?"

The door swung open. "Actually, we keep the bunk-house unlocked. All that's in there is an old foldout couch and a woodstove. If you want to look after Badger, I'll meet you back in here. I want to get the heat going."

It took several minutes for Duke to make sure Badger was comfortable, and then he took his saddle roll and stepped inside the cookhouse. It certainly wasn't fancy—simple construction and wood floors—but it was big. Heavy tables and benches made a line down the middle of the room, ending halfway. The other half of the room held foldout cots topped with gray-and-white-striped mattresses. There was a propane heater and a galley-size kitchen, where Duke could see a propane stove and icebox.

"Wow. This place is bigger than it looks outside."

Carrie laughed, the sound echoing to the bare rafters. "It won't feel so big when there's ten of us sleeping in here together. Jimmy snores. Did I remember to tell you to bring earplugs?"

He laughed, too. He'd spent enough time in barracks to be immune to that sort of thing.

Carrie continued talking as she lit the propane stove. "One of these days it's going to need a new roof and some repairs. Things are getting a little creaky."

He stomped off his boots and then stepped farther inside. "Why didn't Joe look after that?"

"It was on his list for next year. He was an old man, Duke. He didn't have the energy that he used to."

She started taking off her jacket. The heater was working and the air immediately around it began to warm. "Put your roll on a bed," she suggested. "Boss man gets first dibs."

"What about the foreman?"

"I already picked mine."

Sure enough, her roll was sitting atop the bed closest to the heater. Smarty. "I guess that gives me second dibs," he countered, and dropped his roll on a nearby cot.

A few of the men enjoyed a smoke outside before coming in, while others entered, dropped their rolls and took time for a nature break. Duke stayed inside with Carrie. She set out paper plates and bowls, plastic cutlery, paper cups and napkins while Duke manhandled two pots and put them on the flaming burners. Carrie had said that in the past, Joe had supplied the men with sandwiches and coffee the night before the drive, but he wanted to have something more substantial. He'd put on his chef's hat and put together a huge batch of chili, and he'd bought bags of buns at the bakery. Tonight the men would come inside and have a hot meal and then in the morning there'd be a feed of bacon and eggs before they headed out to move the herd back to the main ranch.

He lifted a lid to give the chili a stir. When he put the spoon down, he caught Carrie watching him. "What?" he asked.

"I'm impressed. I never pegged you as a cook."

"You haven't tasted it yet," he pointed out.

"It smells good."

"The thing with chili is that it's okay I made it Wednesday night. It's better if it sits for a day or so."

"It might make for loud bed partners tonight," she joked, waggling her eyebrows. She went to work slicing and buttering buns to go with the chili.

Duke watched her and wondered what it was like to be the sole female in a crew of men. It didn't seem to bother her, but he knew for a fact that men could be rough. He hadn't needed to be in the army very long before he realized that manners didn't matter much.

"Do you ever find it difficult?" he asked, watching her put the buttered buns back in the bag.

"What's that?" she replied, putting the cover back on the margarine container.

"The guys. I mean you're like one of them, but you're a lady."

"Are you saying I'm not qualified, Duke?"

"Not at all." He'd been watching her all week, learning from her. She was smart and she was dedicated to the ranch, put up with no nonsense but knew how to have a laugh. "The men like and respect you. I just wondered if you personally find it a challenge."

"Not at Crooked Valley. Sometimes elsewhere, though, when I'm dealing with other operations or new people at the stockyards. I try to work it to my advantage."

He nodded. "I've been watching and learning the past few weeks. I don't know a lot about the ins and outs of raising cattle, but I can see that you know what you're doing. Quinn thinks a lot of you."

"Quinn's a good guy. Smart, easygoing but fiscally conservative. I've heard Joe say that when times got tight, it was Quinn who saved the ranch from being hit as hard as it might have been. You couldn't do better for a teacher."

Duke took a step closer to her. "Funny," he said softly, his gaze drawn to her full lips. "He said the same about you."

"Duke…"

"I know." He didn't move away, even though he heard the warning in her tone when she said his name. "The problem is, I can't get last Friday out of my head. I don't know why."

"Because I turned you down?"

He laughed, enjoying her bluntness. "Maybe. You definitely left me wanting more."

"Which we both agreed would be a mistake."

"So you haven't been thinking about it?"

He watched her cheeks color. She didn't need to say the words for him to have his answer.

"Here's the thing," Duke mused. "I stopped because you asked me to. And because you'd been drinking and I didn't want you to come back and accuse me of taking advantage."

Fire lit her eyes. "I wouldn't do that! I knew exactly what I was doing."

He knew that. The way she'd taken control in the truck had been enough for him to realize she knew her own mind.

The men were still out on the porch. Duke could hear them talking and laughing, and he took the opportunity to move even closer to Carrie. "What are we going to do about this, then?" he asked softly, lifting his hand a smoothing back a piece of her hair that had come loose from her low ponytail.

"This what?" she asked, but her voice took on a breathy quality that made his blood run faster. It was the same husky tone she'd used when she'd told him to scoot over on the seat—just before she'd straddled him.

"This," he answered, and moved the last few inches to kiss her.

There was a moment of surprise where her mouth froze beneath his, but then she thawed, leaning into the kiss. He found himself grateful that she was a forthright woman, because there was no shyness in the way she kissed. She met him halfway, molding her lips to his, meeting his tongue with her own. Desire roared through him as he reached out and pulled her close against his body.

There was a loud thump outside the door and a burst of laughter and they jumped, pulling apart.

"You have to stop doing that!" she hissed, frowning and taking a step backward. "What if one of the guys walked in? You say I'm respected with the crew, but how do you think that would hold up if they thought I was messing around with the hot new boss?"

"You think I'm hot?" He smiled a little. When they were in an enclosed space like this, he didn't have any trouble hearing her or watching her lips. It was strange how watching her mouth form the words made them clearer somehow. Only inches separated them. She was crystal clear. And she'd definitely called him hot.

"That's not what I meant!"

"That's what you said."

"Stir your chili so it doesn't stick to the bottom."

He chuckled. "We're not going to be able to ignore it forever, you know. But you're right. We should probably keep it private. For appearances."

"Duke. We can't do this."

He met her gaze evenly. "Give me one good reason why not. And don't say because you work for me. We've covered that."

Consternation twisted her features, and she reached out and grabbed the wooden spoon, lifting one of the lids and stirring the contents of the pot. Duke reached out and covered her hand with his. "One good reason," he insisted.

She stared up at him, but remained silent.

"That's what I thought."

He turned away, but she reached out and grabbed his arm, making him turn back again. "I can give you three. Because we're too different," she answered, her mouth tight. "Because you don't even know if you're staying. And because I have enough to lose without getting involved with you, too."

The door to the cookhouse opened and two of the men stomped in, rubbing their hands together and talking, preventing Duke from responding. Not that he knew what to say. He retreated to the other side of the kitchen and took a heavy plastic container of cookies out of a storage box. As everyone eventually made their way inside, Duke filled a huge kettle with water and put it on a back burner to heat for coffee.

She was right. He didn't know what the future held and it was frustrating. Carrie simply didn't understand that in a split second, his choices had been taken away. He'd lost half his hearing and he'd been handed a medical discharge. He hadn't wanted the ranch but it had been put upon him anyway, and now he was responsible for it. No one had bothered to ask what he wanted. It just was, and by God from now on he'd do the choosing— including whether he stayed or not.

Carrie put on her jacket and claimed she had to use the facilities.

She was trying to get away from him, but it wouldn't work for long. The attraction between them was too strong, and more than once Duke had had the feeling that they could both use the release. Carrie was wound pretty tight and so was he. Several times he'd had the feeling he was building up a head of steam and one of these days it was going to erupt.

But that wasn't going to happen tonight. Besides, there were eight other men who were going to be crammed in the cookhouse on army cots. Not as if they'd have any privacy.

"Okay, boys, come and get it," he called out. The resulting clamor as the crew lined up for chow made him feel strangely at home. He missed the army. Missed his old life. Maybe for tonight he should just be glad for the chance to revisit that feeling for a little while.

CARRIE TRIED TO keep her movements quiet inside her sleeping bag. It made the tiniest rustle as she shifted her weight. As far as she could tell, she was the only one awake this early. It was still full-on dark outside, but the moon illuminated the room in an angled beam through the back window of the cookhouse. There was just enough light for her to make out Duke's face, restful in sleep, on the cot across from her.

She'd watched him most of the evening. The smile that had been so reluctant at the bar came easier out here as the men talked and joked with each other. The food had been tasty and there'd been some good-natured teasing about keeping him on as a cook if the boss thing didn't work out. Duke took it all in stride, and he had an endearing way of turning his head to the right just before he laughed. It was, as Joe would've said, Duke's tell.

Now he was sound asleep, and she thought back to the kiss they'd shared today. It troubled her. Every time they got too close or touched, Carrie felt as if she was going to combust. Duke didn't make it easy either, asking stupid questions.

Like demanding one good reason why they shouldn't explore what was between them.

A week ago, maybe it would have been safe. Maybe she should have just gone through with it then and got Duke Duggan out of her system. But she hadn't. Instead he'd brought her coffee. Bought her breakfast. Asked for her advice and help. She'd seen him work around the ranch, swallowing his pride and honest to goodness learning from everyone from Quinn down to the part-time teenager who came in after school to work in the horse barn.

He made chili. Played cards with the guys by lamplight and laughed when he lost.

He wanted one good reason? She liked him too much. She liked Duke a whole lot, and sleeping with him would only make it more likely that she'd get hurt. At first she'd thought he was the solution to all their problems. But now...she could see he was troubled. It was in the strange moments of silence and the sober expression on his face when he thought no one was looking. There was more going on with Duke than she suspected most people realized.

She shifted again, but Duke never moved.

Dawn was beginning to lighten the sky when more of the crew began to stir in that peculiar restlessness that happened just before waking. Carrie was just about to swing her legs over the side of the cot and turn the temperature up on the heater when an eerie sound crept out of the darkness.

Coyotes. Dammit.

"You hear that?" a raspy voice whispered from a few cots away.

"Yeah, I heard," she whispered back. "I hope they're not hunting."

"Strange for this time of year. The calves aren't babies anymore." It was Tim's voice, one of the guys from Triple B.

"You folks been having any trouble over at your place?"

"Not so much."

The howl echoed again, followed by some yips and more howling. "I'm hoping moving the herd closer to the main house will solve the problem," she admitted. "Once a coyote gets a taste he keeps coming back. I should've started trapping two weeks ago."

Jack sat up on his cot. "The noise is coming from down by the river. Crap."

Carrie let out a breath and crawled out of the warmth of her sleeping bag. There was more quiet shuffling as the other hands woke.

All except Duke. His head was tucked onto his left hand, and he slept on, oblivious to the noises around him. It was as though he couldn't even hear the howling or the sounds of the nylon sleeping bags.

Considering she'd been awake since five, she envied him the ability to sleep so soundly.

Now that almost everyone was up, someone turned on a lamp, and shuffling sounds riffled through the space, along with the odd zipper of a jacket or pack. Carrie was just shoving her arms into a flannel shirt when Duke's eyes opened and he stretched his arms over his head. Her gaze was drawn to his long arms and curved shoulders, still in a T-shirt, but it didn't do

much to camouflage his physique. Carrie looked away
and focused on buttoning the shirt over the tank top
she'd slept in.

"What's going on?" His voice was gritty from dis-
use and sexy as hell.

"Coyotes down by the river. The howling woke most
of us up."

"I must've slept soundly." His gaze skittered away
from hers as he responded. He unzipped his sleeping
bag and crawled out.

He'd removed his jeans and had slept in his long
underwear—not the thick thermal kind either, but tight-
fitting athletic wear in solid black. The fabric skimmed
and clung to the muscles in his legs and she tried not to
stare. Then he stood up, gave a little hobble and winced.

She managed a chuckle. "Long ride yesterday, huh."

He nodded. "Longer one today."

"You're going to need a long soak in a hot tub by tonight," she warned him, grinning. "Tenderfoot."

He reached for his pants at the foot of his cot, the
motion putting them slightly closer together. "You joining me?" he asked quietly, his voice low and intimate.

Heat rushed to her cheeks. "Stop doing that."

"Sorry." His tone was anything but contrite.

"Hey, Carrie. You want a couple of us to ride out
and see what's up?"

"I'll come with you," she said, turning her back on
Duke's seductive eyes.

"Do you need help?" Duke asked, coming to stand
by her shoulder.

She only half turned toward him. "Naw, a few of us
is all we need. They guys know what to do. We'll have
breakfast and pack up and be on the go soon. Just save
me some bacon, okay?"

Within minutes three of them were saddling up their mounts and heading down toward the riverbed. As they approached the cattle, they could sense the agitation in the herd. Several animals were clumped together in a protective group. Riding farther on, Carrie spotted blood on the fresh snow, along with mud and dirt where hooves had churned up the grass beneath in their hurry to escape.

The animal hadn't escaped. Neither had it been killed. They found the heifer several yards away, down on the ground, wounded and gasping for breath.

Carrie swallowed thickly. She guessed their approach had scared the pack away, or they would have finished the job. A nearly grown cow was harder to bring down than a new calf, and they'd never had this problem before. The animal had to be stopped. When she got back to the ranch, she'd talk to Quinn about setting some traps. Coyotes were a way of life here, but an aggressive hunter was a big problem.

She dismounted and reached for the gun she always carried when she was out this far. Saliva pooled in her mouth as her stomach churned. Randy, one of the men who'd come along, put his hand on her arm.

"You want me to do this?" he asked quietly.

"Naw. I've got it." She handed him Sage's reins. This was not the part of the job she relished, but she couldn't watch the poor animal suffer, either. She walked over to the cow, clicked off the safety, took aim and fired.

The herd shifted restlessly again as the shot echoed through the valley. The men were respectfully quiet as she slid the rifle back into place and mounted up.

"Keep your eyes open," she instructed the men. "If you see any animal from that pack, shoot it."

"Yes, ma'am."

But there was no glimpse of grayish-brown hair, no howls or yips to indicate the pack was close by.

The sky was much brighter when they returned to camp, and Carrie took some extra time looking after Sage while Randy and Jack followed the smell of bacon and coffee. It wasn't until they were gone that she let go and rested her head on Sage's warm hide.

It was her job. She wouldn't be much of a foreman if she left the tough tasks to the men. She'd had to earn respect, and now she had to keep it. And in her heart she knew that heifer was far better off, out of its pain and suffering.

But she hated taking a life of any sort.

"Hey, you okay?"

Duke's voice came from behind her and she quickly sniffed and wiped her nose on the side of her glove. "I'm fine. Cold out. Makes my nose run."

A cup of coffee appeared in her peripheral vision. "It's cold out. Warm up," he instructed. "Your nose is running."

She peeled off her gloves and accepted the cup, the heat welcome against her chilled fingers. "Thanks," she said, but frowned a little. Had he not heard her comment on the cold or her nose?

He came around to her right side. "Jack said you took the shot."

"Yeah."

"Maybe I should watch my p's and q's around you a bit more."

She couldn't help but smile at his obvious attempt to tease. "Maybe you should," she answered, but her shoulders relaxed a little.

"Come in and have some breakfast," Duke suggested. "You'll feel better."

She turned to face him fully. "How did you do it, Duke? How did you handle being in the army, being deployed, having to fire on...on other human beings?" She couldn't ask him if he'd ever killed anyone. She didn't think she wanted to know.

"I don't know how to answer that." His gray eyes delved into hers. "You just do. It's your job. And if someone fires on you..."

Of course. You're going to fire back. She knew that in her head. But if she had such a difficult time shooting a cow, she knew she could never stare down the barrel at another person. In that moment, Duke seemed very much like a stranger to her. He'd lived a life she could never understand, so perhaps she shouldn't expect him to understand hers so quickly.

"Come on," he said, turning away. "The drive isn't going to wait all morning. You need to fuel up."

"I'll be right there. I'm going to see if I have any hope of cell coverage out here. I don't like leaving the carcass. We might be able to haul it out with the quad."

"Don't be long," Duke admonished, and as he walked away Carrie felt, for the first time, that she'd just been spoken to by her boss.

Chapter Six

After little to no sleep the night before and a grueling day in the saddle, the last thing Carrie felt like doing was heading to the party at Crooked Valley. The hot bath had been so relaxing she'd nearly nodded off, saved only by the shrill ringing of her phone. Kailey had called to see if she wanted a ride, but Carrie had declined. She was tired and wanted to be able to leave when she was ready. At this rate, that would be right after the meal.

Now she was carrying a casserole and dragging her butt to the big house, the welcoming lights shining through the windows and the sound of laughter echoing through the air as the front door opened and closed. She stopped for a second and thought of Joe, and how much she'd missed him the past few days. He'd loved this event and looked forward to it every year.

But Joe was gone and Duke was here and life went on. She climbed the steps and opened the door, assaulted by laughter, music and the welcoming scent of a down-home potluck guaranteed to please.

Kailey bounced over. "It's about time you got here! We're going to start eating soon. What'd you bring anyway?" Unstoppable, Kailey lifted the foil on top of Carrie's dish and started laughing at the sight of the hash brown casserole. "Funeral potatoes? Seriously?"

Carrie scowled. "Hey. Everyone likes them and it was something I could put together ahead of time and heat up. I've been a bit busy, you know."

Kailey frowned. "Jeez. Lighten up. Rough day?"

Carrie blew out a breath. "Sorry. I'm just tired. I didn't get much sleep out at the camp last night and the coyotes had me up early."

She moved to the long banquet table set out in the dining room and put down her casserole with the others. Her stomach growled in response to the sight and smell of the delicious food—sliced ham, baked beans, short ribs in a Crock-Pot, simmered slowly so that the meat was sure to fall clean off the bone. There was shredded pork and buns, coleslaw, salads and enough pies to fill a baker's shelf.

Kailey put a hand on her shoulder. "Let out a breath and enjoy the evening. Tomorrow's a day off, right?"

Except tomorrow Carrie really wanted to get moving on solving their predator problem. Kailey knew as well as anyone that there really were no days off on a ranch. And because Carrie understood her friend was just trying to make her feel better, she put on a smile and did what Kailey said. She let out a long, restorative breath.

And she would have felt more relaxed had Duke not come through the dining room door at that precise moment.

He'd cleaned up all right. He wore new jeans and a soft navy shirt and his face still had that just-shaved look. His hair had grown out a bit in the few weeks since his arrival and she had been right—it was a glorious auburn. Worse, he looked up at her and she realized the deep navy of his shirt made his gray eyes even more striking.

He weaved his way through the people hovering inside the doorway and made his way over. "You made it," he said loudly, grinning down at her, nodding at Kailey. "I wasn't sure you would."

"I wouldn't miss it," she replied.

"I'm sorry?" He leaned down a little more. Between the music and the people it was loud, but not that loud, at least Carrie didn't think so.

"I said, I wouldn't miss it. Joe loved this event."

He nodded. "It's a bit loud and crazy."

"Maybe you should start the eating. Full mouths are quiet mouths." She laughed a little, her fatigue slipping away.

"How do I do that? Whistle? Shout?"

Carrie laughed and beckoned with a finger. "Come with me, I'll show you."

She led him through to the pantry and retrieved an old iron triangle. "Your grandmother used this to round up the folks." It was quieter in the pantry, and she lowered her voice to a normal volume. "You should do the honors. It's tradition."

"Isn't it a little cliché?"

"Would you rather shout?"

He grinned. "Good point."

She handed him the striker. "Go to it, cowboy."

They headed back to the main area of the house and Carrie stood aside while Duke rang the bell. Conversation instantly dropped off and he chuckled. "Well, how about that?" he mused, looking over at her and smiling.

"Joe used to give a blessing," she prompted. But Duke looked uncomfortable, so she leaned forward. "Maybe you could ask Quinn to do it."

He nodded, reassured. "Hey, folks, welcome to Crooked Valley. I'm new to all these traditions, and we've got a lot of food to plow through here, so maybe Quinn would lead us in saying grace and we can get started?" He looked at Quinn hopefully.

"Sure," Quinn agreed. His daughter, Amber, was in his arms looking cute in jeans, a soft pink sweater and blond pigtails. "What do you say, honey?"

Amber nodded. "The one Mommy taught me, okay, Daddy?"

Carrie's throat tightened. Quinn was doing such a good job as a single dad. Amber was the sweetest girl ever.

Together they said grace. "God is great, God is good, thank You, Father, for this food. Amen."

There was a silence afterward, as if everyone was touched by the simple but sweet blessing by the motherless girl.

"Okay, now dig in!" Carrie stepped forward and broke the silence and conversation erupted again as a line started to form by the buffet table.

Duke took the triangle back to the pantry. "God, she's a sweet kid, isn't she?"

Carrie nodded. "She really is. It hasn't been easy on Quinn."

"He said his wife died suddenly a little over a year ago."

"She had some sort of heart defect that no one knew about. Got up to go running one morning and never came home. It was a real shock."

Duke shook his head. "It never makes sense to me, you know? How some people can be in dangerous positions all the time and come out okay, and other people just go about their daily lives and poof. Game over."

"Like you, Duke?"

His face took on a strange impression. "I suppose."

"Well, none of us has the answers to the universe. But I know Kailey brought those short ribs and they are delicious. Let's go eat and solve the world's problems later."

They joined the group and Carrie filled her plate with so much food she knew she couldn't possibly eat it all. The noise quieted to a dull roar punctuated with laughter and she sat and talked with the wives and girlfriends of the Crooked Valley and Triple B hands.

She noticed Duke setting up a big garbage can for the refuse and got up to help. The coffee was ready, so she poured it into a carafe and started another pot while people helped themselves to dessert. They crossed paths as she was going to the sink to wash spoons and spatulas.

"You don't have to do that," he said. "I can get it later."

"I don't suppose you're used to playing host," she replied. "And you're doing this all alone after a busy day. I don't mind. I know where things go."

It was quieter in the kitchen and they worked together for a while. Then the other women kicked it into gear as they tidied up the food and put covers back on their casseroles and Tupperware. Before long the dining room was spick-and-span, the folding banquet table stored away, and someone turned up the volume on the music. Quinn took Amber and went home. The noise level rose again, the front door kept opening and closing and Carrie felt her exhaustion come trickling back. Maybe it was time to go.

And then she saw Duke slip out the back door to

the veranda. His face looked tight, as though he was annoyed.

What had happened?

She followed him out to the porch, carefully shutting the door behind her.

"Duke?"

He didn't respond, so she went up behind him and touched his shoulder. He spun around so fast he nearly knocked her over.

"Whoa," she said, taking a step back. "I didn't mean to scare you. Didn't you hear me come outside?"

That strange look shadowed his face again and something twisted in Carrie's stomach. "What is it, Duke? Every now and again you get this look on your face. Pained and a little angry. Did I do something wrong?"

He turned away and rested his hands on the railing.

It was cold, and Carrie folded her arms around herself. Maybe she should just turn around and go back inside. She didn't need to get caught up in Duke's drama, whatever it was. She had enough of her own worries, both professional and personal.

So why was she still standing here?

"You're so stubborn," she muttered, and Duke spun back around, frustration rippling off him as he faced her.

"I can't understand you when you mumble like that," he snapped.

"I wasn't mumbling."

"Well, you sure weren't being clear. If you have something to say, say it."

She was tired and had come out here to help and he was biting her head off. "Fine," she snapped back. "You're a stubborn…" She fought for the right word. "Ass! Clear enough for you?"

Her hands were on her hips and she had her chin up. Duke was glaring down at her, his eyes shooting sparks. And then suddenly they started laughing, down low. "Feel better?" he asked, softer now, and she nodded.

"I think I do, yes," she replied. "Duke, what's going on with you? Half the time I get the feeling you don't realize I exist. You don't hear me or you pass by without acknowledging me. The other half of the time I feel like I'm the sole focus of your attention. It's weird."

For a long moment his troubled eyes held hers. "I... Oh, this is stupid," he said, turning away.

"You what?" She went forward and stood beside him at the railing. The fields beyond were dark, but stars sparkled in the inky depths of the sky. There were no streetlights out here, nothing to disturb the natural nighttime beyond the carriage lamps on either side of Duke's door, casting small circles of light that didn't reach far at all.

He didn't answer, but she got the sense he wanted to. Behind them, inside, the music thumped along and muffled voices drifted out now and then. Goose bumps popped up on Carrie's arms and she figured she might as well go back inside where it was warm when he finally spoke.

"I don't always hear so well," he admitted.

Hearing? Whatever she'd thought he might answer, it wasn't that. "What do you mean?"

He didn't look at her, just stared out into the darkness. "Right now I can hear you just fine because you're standing on my left. If you were on my right, I might not have known you spoke. Or I would have heard you say something, but not been able to tell what it was."

He let out a heavy sigh. "I've lost almost all my hearing in my right ear."

She turned her head and looked up at him. "How? I mean, when?"

"A few months ago. When I was wounded."

Her stomach took a sharp dip. "Wait, you were wounded?"

He finally looked over at her. "Did you think I got bored of the army and just left?"

"I don't know. I didn't want to ask. But you didn't look…"

"Disabled?"

"You're not disabled," she replied staunchly. "Look at you. You're in great shape, you're…"

"Hearing loss is a disability. There's no two ways around it, Carrie. It makes me unable to do what I love to do and that's why I left the army. If that's not a disability, what is?"

The bitterness was obvious in his voice. "You mean in combat, right? But surely there are other areas within the army…"

"Yeah, no, thanks," he said bitterly. "There's no place for me in the sandbox. Or in combat in general." He shrugged his shoulders. "Can you see me sitting at a desk or a warehouse somewhere?"

She couldn't. Even though he'd known little about ranching when he arrived and had only scraped the surface of what it entailed, she could see that Duke was happiest when he was outside, busy, vital. Anything else would be like caging him up.

She got it. She felt the same way about the ranch. What if something happened that she had to say goodbye not only to Crooked Valley but her occupation altogether? No wonder he hadn't smiled much when he got here. But he'd been smiling more lately….

"Why didn't you say anything earlier?"

"I can still hear out of my left ear, and I didn't want to answer questions."

"Oh." More like he didn't want to show any bit of weakness. Or really let anyone in. In her line of work she knew what it was to have pride, but she also knew a man had a special brand of pride that sometimes caused tunnel vision. "Sorry I asked."

"That's not what I meant." He faced her now. "I just didn't want all of Gibson to know." He frowned. "The last thing I ever want to hear is 'poor Duke.'"

"You won't hear it from me."

The air around them relaxed a little. "Thank you for that."

"Hey, I've had my fair share of poor Carrie comments. I understand."

Indeed she had. After her mother had taken ill, after her father died, after Logan had taken off only three weeks after their engagement…

Poor Carrie.

And then Duke had arrived and turned everything upside down. She frowned and looked up into his face. "So those times you went by me and didn't say anything—you really didn't hear me say hello?"

He shook his head.

"And the coyotes last night?"

"I was sleeping on my left side. Good ear in the pillow, can't hear anything out of my right."

Something else twigged. "Is that why you stare at me when I talk to you?"

His cheeks colored a bit in the dim light. "Yeah. I seem to be able to hear things more clearly when I can watch people's lips move."

As interesting as that little tidbit was, what Carrie felt most was disappointment. All the times she'd felt

he was so attentive, so interested…he'd just been trying
to understand her better. She wasn't so special after all.

"Oh."

Duke let out a breath and seemed relieved; he didn't
appear to clue in to Carrie's disappointment. Which
was probably a good thing when all was said and done.
She'd read more into things than she should—it wasn't
the first time.

"I know I should go back inside," she heard him say,
"but all the voices and the noise… It's hard to separate out the strands and hear just one thing. It kind of
becomes a jumble, and then I get tense and frustrated
and a bit overwhelmed. I needed to get outside and get
some space for a bit."

Translation: he'd come out here to be alone. And
she'd followed him out here like the Brandt's farm dog
followed at Kailey's heels. Devoted and dumb. What
a fool she was.

"I'd better get back inside." He couldn't have made
it plainer, and she might as well go home. Get a good
night's sleep. Start exercising some common sense
where Duke was concerned.

He reached out and grabbed her arm. "I didn't mean
you, Carrie." They were face-to-face now and that stupid spark flared to life again.

"You said you wanted space…."

"From the noise. From the crowd. Not from you."

And then it dawned. That night at the bar, how focused he'd looked, how he didn't smile much. The hum
of chaos must have been unreal between the music and
the shouted conversations. When he'd gone out to his
truck, he'd been looking to get away from the noise and
the crowd. But not from her.

She shivered, and only half of the reason was the

cold. "Duke, you have to let me go. Anyone could look out here and see us. Not a big deal when we were just talking, but this…"

She knew how it must look. They were only inches apart, his hand on her arm, her looking up into his handsome face…

He let go of her arm.

"Don't go home," he said. "Stay. For a while."

"Duke…"

"Other than Quinn, you're the one I know best. And Quinn's gone home. I wouldn't mind having a—"

"Wingman?" she suggested, smiling a little.

"Yeah."

"Duke, can I be honest?"

"Of course you can." He was focused on her face again, but now she knew it was so he could understand her better. She toyed with the words sitting on her lips. Questions about what had happened to him. Wondering if he'd asked her back to his place because of this thing between them or if he meant what he said about it being platonic. Wondering what he'd say if she told him what was really on her mind—mainly wishing she had never turned him away that night at her house.

She blinked and said simply, "I'm freezing."

"I guess we'd better go in, then."

They were nearly to the door when Duke's voice stopped her again. "Carrie? Don't tell anyone about this, okay?"

She wasn't sure she was a big fan of holding on to his secrets, but he'd confided in her and he deserved her discretion in return for his trust. "Your secret is safe with me," she answered, and put her hand on the door handle.

Inside the noise enveloped her once more, as well as

the welcome warmth. But she heard it a little bit differently now, wondering what it must be like for Duke, and wondering why he was so secretive about it. He'd said it happened when he was wounded, but nothing more. What had really gone down the day he'd been hurt? Did that have something to do with why he didn't talk about it?

She smiled and circulated through the remaining guests, but the whole time she was thinking that Duke was more of a mystery now than he had been when he first arrived.

Chapter Seven

He couldn't believe he'd told her.

Came right out and admitted he was half-deaf. Blame it on a moment of weakness, maybe. He was tired, the noise had become overwhelming, and there she'd been, quiet and pretty, standing on his porch with the stars overhead...

He'd trusted her. He'd confided in her. And that went well beyond the physical need that had been driving him up to this point. Maybe it was her own troubles in the past that made her seem like someone who could understand.

And yet he hated revealing that weakness to anyone. He wished he hadn't done it. It was bad enough that everyone in his employ knew more about ranching than he did. Add in his deafness... He was sure they all expected him to fail.

Now the last of the partyers was going home, most of the mess was already cleaned up and Carrie was reaching for her jacket.

Trouble was, even though he was tired, he was too keyed up to sleep and he knew it. It had something to do with being overstimulated, but some nights it took hours for him to relax enough to fall into a decent sleep. What he needed right now was some downtime to catch his breath. And he didn't enjoy the thought of going back to his place alone.

"Hey, do you want a glass of wine or something?" He followed Carrie to the hall. "I'm going to chill for a while. Wouldn't mind some company. There's probably a late-night show coming on soon."

"It's been a long day," Carrie replied. "I've been awake since before five."

"Right." And he didn't want to seem desperate. But damn. As fun as the neighbors had been—despite the noise—he was lonely. This was so far removed from the life he'd known for years.

"Besides, I have to drive home."

"You could always crash here." At her alarmed look, he continued, "There are lots of beds here at the house. And I'm in the bunkhouse. It's no biggie."

Her knuckles were nearly white as they gripped her casserole dish. "And my car would be in the yard overnight. It's a small town, Duke."

"Who's going to see it? You can't even see the house from the road."

"Quinn. The hands when they come in the morning to look after the stock."

"So you tell them that you left your car here. No biggie."

She hesitated, which meant either she was trying to come up with another excuse or she actually wanted to stay and was considering it.

"Come on. When was the last time you just hung out, had a drink, watched some TV? I get a little tired of doing that alone."

"You just want to hang out?"

Hell no. Just last night he'd kissed her in the cook-house kitchen, and as he recalled there'd been a suggestion about a hot bath for two at some point. It was the strangest thing. Duke usually went for the stereotypically pretty girls who dressed in nice clothes and wore makeup and were, well, girlie. But Carrie was different. She was pretty in a more natural way. She didn't need fancy clothes or eyeliner or hot rollers or whatever women used to get themselves dolled up. Besides, he found her independence and capabilities really attractive. There was something inherently sexy about her strength and confidence.

"Sure," he answered, mentally calling himself a big fat liar. "Just hang out."

She seemed to ponder a moment more, then nodded. "Okay. But not wine. You have any beer at your place?"

He nearly choked on a laugh. They were peas in a pod, weren't they? Maybe Carrie would be easier to resist if he didn't actually like her so much.

"I think there's a few in the fridge," he answered.

They walked across the frosty yard, stars glittering sharply in the cold, clear night. Their boots made crunching sounds on the hard gravel and snow, and Duke found himself wondering what she was thinking.

The inside of the bunkhouse was warm, and they shivered out of their jackets. "I'm going to add some wood to the fire," he said, heading straight for the living room, where a black woodstove sat on a brick base. "Why don't you grab us a few beers?"

He turned the damper up, then opened the door and shoved in three sticks of wood from the rack beside the stove. When the bark caught, he shut the door again, waiting for the fire to really get going before turning the damper again.

When he stood, Carrie was waiting for him, holding

out a bottle of beer. "It's nice in here," she commented. "I haven't been inside in a while."

He nodded. "I don't think anyone was. It was pretty dirty and neglected. But it's much more my size."

"Quinn lived here for a while, a long time ago now. Then he got married and they bought a bigger house." She met his gaze. "A family house." She didn't have to say any more. He could tell they were both thinking about Quinn and his adorable daughter and how he was now bringing her up on his own.

Duke led the way to the sofa and sat down, waiting for Carrie to follow his lead. When she sat on the opposite side of the sofa, he picked up the remote and turned on the TV. The last minutes of a hockey game were on and for a bit they watched until the horn sounded and the third period was over.

And all the while he was aware of her sitting next to him, a respectable space between them, looking young and pretty and accepting him for exactly who he was. He sipped at his beer and let his gaze fall on her. He'd been so nervous about revealing his injury to anyone, but Carrie had brushed it off. Not to make it seem like nothing, but to let him know that it didn't matter.

His hearing loss was now part of who he was. For weeks he'd thought that made him less of a person somehow. That people would look at him differently. But Carrie hadn't made him feel like anything was missing. She made him feel like he just…was. Duke Duggan. What you see is what you get.

It was a revelation. He doubted she understood how much.

"Are you going to stare at me all night?" she asked quietly, her gaze never leaving the television screen.

"Sorry." He spared a glance at the TV, which had

switched to some late-night infomercial for a revolution-
ary cooking utensil. He smiled and nodded at the screen.
"Are you saying that's more interesting than I am?"

She looked over at him and the connection hit him
in the chest and stole his breath.

Her pupils widened slightly. "And that's why I didn't
look at you," she murmured. "What are we going to
do about this, Duke? We can't...we shouldn't...and yet
every time we get together it's like..."

"Fireworks," he said hoarsely. "And I'm running out
of willpower, Carrie. I thought we could just hang out.
I thought it would take away the quiet. But there's no
'just' anything with you. I don't know why."

"Me, either."

The admission only heightened the tension between
them. "You've got to know," he said, his gaze never
leaving hers, "that I can't think past tomorrow. I don't
know what my future holds. I don't have plans, I can't
make promises. If I offer you tonight, that's what this
is. Tonight. I don't want you pinning hopes on me."

God, he could just about drown in her eyes.

"I gave up pinning hopes on people long ago," she
replied. "It's just easier that way."

It was a good answer for a man like him, so he wasn't
sure why it unsettled him so. He tried to push it to the
back of his mind. "So what are we going to do about
this, then? About...us?"

She didn't answer. The television announcer babbled
on about how life would be so much easier and better
if you only bought what he was selling. Duke wished it
was that easy. Give a credit card number over the phone
and your life's problems solved. A piece of cake when
someone else knew what you needed and gave it to you,
instead of having to painfully figure it out for yourself.

One of them had to make the first move—either to be together or push away. He really didn't know which would take more strength.

"Duke," she said softly, and that one word broke the thread of his control. She was feeling it, too. The pull. The need. The inevitability.

"Come here." He took the remote and muted the volume, so only the light from the screen flashed through the room.

Once again he was surprised at her obedience. She put down her still-full bottle on the coffee table and scooted across the cushions until she was seated beside him, half-turned so they were facing each other. She'd put her hair up again and he reached behind and slid the elastic away from the soft strands, sinking his fingers into the heavy golden mass. The underside was still damp from her bath, and the scent of her shampoo rose up in a perfumed cloud.

"I don't want to take this fast," he murmured, leaning closer and touching his lips to the velvety softness of her earlobe. "I don't want it over too soon."

Her breath touched his cheek, warm and shaky. "Okay."

He smiled against the skin of her jaw. "It's been…a while," he admitted. Quite a while. After the breakup, he'd let the guys convince him to go out a few times, hook up. It wasn't his style and it had got old real fast. Truth be told, Duke rather suspected he was a one-woman kind of man.

Which meant he shouldn't even be considering what he was about to do. Not if he had no intention of it going any further.

"It's been a while for me, too," she confessed.

When he touched his lips to hers, he had to fight for

control. His body was screaming for a wild, button-popping, clothes-ripping, frenzied coupling. While it would be ultimately satisfying, it would be over too quickly. It took all his willpower to move slowly, kiss her thoroughly, to gentle his hands on her skin as they fell into an embrace.

Breaths mingled; buttons were undone, clothes removed with soft whispers of fabric on skin. With a gentleness he hadn't known he possessed, he laid her down on the rug in front of the woodstove and lavished his attention on her, nearly breaking his tenuous hold on self-control when she arched beneath him and called out his name.

But when she released a long, satisfied sigh and smiled at him, he was lost. And he didn't regain control until they were side by side on the rug, utterly spent.

SHE SHOULD GO HOME.

Carrie lay in the circle of Duke's arms, covered with a soft afghan he'd pulled off the sofa. The woodstove chugged out a steady heat and between that and the warmth of Duke's body, she was definitely feeling lazy and sleepy.

It might also have something to do with the fabulous sex they'd just had.

But she couldn't stay all night. Duke had said it himself. He couldn't think beyond tomorrow, and they had no business getting involved emotionally. This *thing* between them was just physical. It was satisfying a need that had gone unsatisfied for far too long. Now that they'd done it—and well enough that her body felt quite beautifully boneless—she really needed to gather up her clothes and go back to her own house.

In a minute. Or five.

"Wow," Duke whispered against her hair. "That was…wow."

She chuckled, a soft little vibration inside her chest. "You seem to have misplaced your vocabulary."

"How would you describe what just happened?"

She rose up on an elbow and looked down into his face. God, he was beautiful. Not in a pretty-boy kind of way but in a rough-and-ready, rugged-yet-tender kind of way.

Crap. She was in bigger trouble than she'd thought.

"Wow," she echoed, and his smile grew, making her warm all over.

He closed his eyes and let out a replete sigh. "Told ya," he said, and she smiled.

"Unfortunately, I really should get home. The last thing I need to do is fall asleep here on the floor." Naked. Under a blanket. It sounded deliciously out of character for her. Still, she'd meant what she said earlier. She had to keep the respect of the people she worked with, and she couldn't do that if she and Duke were carrying on.

"We could move to my bed. It's much more comfortable."

And she was tempted. But at some point good sense needed to prevail. "And that's an attractive offer. You also promised me hanging out."

"Yeah, we were both fooling ourselves about that, weren't we?" He brushed off her accusation by sharing the blame. She knew he was right. The hanging-out thing had only been an excuse. A justification. Deep down they'd both known what would happen.

"Well, now that we've, uh, scratched our itch, it's time to get back to business. And for that I really do need to get a good night's sleep, Duke."

He looked up at her, his eyes communicating dark intentions. "And if you stay here, there won't be much sleeping."

She nearly ached with wanting to stay. But it would be a mistake, so she pushed off the afghan and got up to find her clothes. Even with the heat from the stove, goose bumps popped up on her skin.

Duke's grin as he looked at her was lethal.

A blush heated her cheeks as she stepped into her panties and reached for her bra.

"It must be all the manual labor," he mused, sitting up, the afghan pooling around his hips. "But you have got muscles in all the right places. That's very hot."

"You don't have to say that now," she teased, trying to cover her embarrassment. "You already got into my pants."

"Don't do that." His brow furrowed. "Don't put it that way."

"It's okay, Duke. We both know that's what it was. We agreed."

She pulled on her jeans and top and sat on the sofa for a moment. "This doesn't change anything, okay? You're still my boss. You're still sorting things out and I have a job to do. Like you said, you can't look past tomorrow. Neither can I."

She was getting to be a very accomplished liar because, while every word was the truth, she still knew there was a corner of her heart that wished he'd contradict her. How stupid was that?

"You're the most independent woman I've ever known," he said, resting back on his elbows. "Most women would be wondering when we'd see each other again or if things were okay."

"I'm not most women. Besides, I'll see you tomorrow when I come to work."

"Right."

To her chagrin, he got up from the floor and she got a fine view before he grabbed his jeans and pulled them on—without the benefit of underwear. "You sure you don't want to stay, Carrie?"

If he only knew how tempting that offer was, but no. "I only had a few sips out of my beer, and the last thing I want is to do the walk of shame through the farmyard in the morning. It's the right thing, Duke."

"If you're sure…"

"I'm positive."

He walked her to the door, waited while she pulled on her boots and took her gloves out of her coat pocket. "Thanks for your help tonight," he offered, and the conversation felt stilted now, talking about the mundane when twenty minutes ago they'd been entwined on the living room floor.

"No problem. And you did good on the drive," she complimented. "We could make a rancher out of you yet."

"We'll see," he said, but there was nothing that sounded of commitment in his voice. Still, he was settling in well. There was still a chance he'd choose to stay. Give Crooked Valley the security it so desperately needed.

One of them had to say goodbye first, so she took a breath and stood on tiptoe, touching her lips lightly to his. "Good night," she murmured, and before he could reply she ducked out his door into the cold night.

The door shut behind her, and she was just turning out of the driveway when she saw the flicker of his porch light turning off.

Chapter Eight

For two weeks Carrie managed to steer clear of any moments alone with Duke. She showed up and did her work and went home again at night. When she did encounter Duke at the ranch, she made sure she was with Quinn or one of the hands—or that he was. No time for personal chats. From that first morning, she was determined to set the tone between them and she did—ruthlessly.

She was firm on it, and she knew it was because being with Duke had affected her more than she cared to admit.

And it had all been going fine until Quinn had come up with this brainiac idea that they should all spend Thanksgiving together since they were at loose ends, family-wise.

Carrie shivered as she entered the barn, the easy gait of her horse swaying her hips back and forth as the hooves clopped on the floor. God, it was cold out there. Another few inches of snow had fallen and right afterward the thermometer had plunged. The good news was the cattle were doing fine and she'd encountered no problems this morning. The bad news was she'd tried trapping the coyote that was giving her trouble and so far—nothing. She wanted to think he'd moved on, but she doubted it. Sooner or later he'd be back for more.

"Everything okay?" Duke's voice came from her right and her head snapped up, startled to see him standing there.

"Yeah. Just cold. Boy, it's freezing. Herd's doing fine, though. This morning they were huddled together down in a coulee, all sheltered and snug."

"Haven't seen you much lately."

She met his gaze. When had he started looking the part of rancher? Today he wore a heavy work jacket, and his chestnut hair was topped by a plain brown Stetson. Her gaze took a trip down his long, denim-clad legs to his worn-in boots. Oh, yeah. The fire still burned in her belly but she paid it no attention. "Been busy."

"Me, too," he replied. "Quinn's been walking me through the bucking stock business. He seems to think we should sell it off. Concentrate the ranch on cattle."

Hmm. Carrie wasn't sure she agreed with that assessment, even if she understood where it was coming from. "That's because Quinn isn't as comfortable with that side of the ranch. It really needs a skilled hand to run it, and right now we can't afford to bring someone in. What are you going to do? You planning on selling it?"

She dismounted and tied the mare while she worked at removing her saddle and blanket.

"I can't. Well, I can, but I need Lacey and Rylan to sign off on it. And I don't want to pressure them right now."

She hefted the saddle and waddled into the tack room to put it away. "You should ask them their plans at dinner tomorrow."

He'd followed her to the tack room door. "I haven't exactly called them yet."

"Still? But you've been here almost a month already. And Thanksgiving is tomorrow." It had only been the idea of Lacey and Rylan being here that had made her agree in the first place. Lots of people. Not so intimate.

"They know where I am."

Stubborn. That was what he was. "What's the deal with you, then? Why don't you talk to your brother and sister? Or your mom? Jeez, Duke, you weren't brought up in a bubble, you know."

"You know, I really appreciate how you don't sugar-coat things on my behalf, Carrie."

She couldn't help but chuckle a little. "I thought you appreciated my honesty."

And then she looked up. All the hard work of the past two weeks—the deliberate timing, excuses, even skipping out on the Triple B potluck—melted away as she looked up into his eyes.

"Excuse me. I need to finish putting up Sage."

He stepped aside and she brushed past him, her pulse hammering. Crap.

"Maybe I should skip tomorrow's dinner," she mused out loud. "Tell Quinn I'm spending it with Kailey's family."

"We can't avoid each other forever. Besides, he's doing it for you, you know."

Her head snapped up. "For me?"

Duke nodded. "Quinn said that Joe always invited you to these things. And that before Gram died, you and your mom always came for holidays. He wanted you to have that in some way this year."

"Quinn said that?" Her mouth dropped open and Sage's bridle dangled in her hand.

"I asked him if he had a thing for you."

Her stomach tumbled around. Why weren't they able to keep any conversation away from romance in some way? "Quinn's like a brother."

"That's what he said. That he's like a big brother and a bit protective where you're concerned."

There was a bite to Duke's tone that made Carrie wonder if Quinn had sensed something going on between Duke and herself. And if he'd made any feelings known about it. Not that she was going to ask.

"So you see," he continued on, "you have to come. Besides, you're on dessert."

Yup. Pumpkin pie she was picking up from the Flour Power Bakery on the way home.

"Right."

She must have sounded put out because Duke came around and took Sage's lead. "Come on, Carrie. It looks to me as though Quinn's the only family you've got. You don't want to let him down just because you're avoiding me."

"Who said I'm avoiding you?" She reached for the lead but he held it away.

"Aren't you? All business. I get it. You think we crossed a line, right? But you'd really hurt Quinn's feelings. And Amber's."

Great. Now he was guilt-tripping her into it. The thing was, it wasn't Quinn she minded thinking about as family. It was Duke. Sitting across the table from him, eating turkey and mashed potatoes and pie and getting used to him being around. It wasn't about the fact they'd slept together. It was because she couldn't stop thinking about him. Couldn't stop having these *feelings* that she neither liked nor wanted. Feelings that she was sure were going to get her hurt in the end.

"Tell you what," she bargained, taking the rope from his hand. "I won't cancel if you call Rylan and Lacey and invite them to join us."

The look on his face was comical.

"Come on, Duke. You don't have to look so constipated about it." She laughed as she led Sage down the corridor to her stall.

"Fine," he called after her. "I'll call them and invite them. It won't matter. They won't come."

He sounded victorious, but she wondered if he really believed his family wouldn't come or if he was in for a big surprise.

THE COLD TREND continued through Thanksgiving and Carrie dressed in neat jeans and a thick red sweater, topped with a warm coat and a knitted scarf wrapped around her neck. She shivered in her truck as it warmed up. The heater wasn't working as well as it could; she wondered if she needed a new thermostat or heater core. Quinn had called this morning, letting her know there would be one extra this afternoon. Lacey had accepted Duke's invitation, though Quinn hadn't said anything about Rylan or Duke's mom.

She'd wait another few seconds to let the engine get warm. To pass the time she flipped down the visor and peered at her reflection in the small mirror. She'd left her hair mostly down today, just pulled back from the sides a bit as the rest of the waves fell free. And she'd put on mascara and lip gloss.... It was a special occasion after all. She was glad now. Not for Duke, of course, but because she'd just bet Lacey was gorgeous and chances were Carrie would feel tomboyish anyway. At least this way she looked as if she'd attempted to be feminine.

The drive to Crooked Valley was beautiful. The sun was peeping through the naked trees, the sky a clear, clear blue. Pinpricks of light glinted off the light covering of snow on the ground. It looked more like

Christmas than Thanksgiving, but Carrie didn't mind. She'd always liked the snow. So had her mom. She sure missed her today. Years past, they'd celebrate Thanksgiving as a family in their little house. It had been happy once, with the three of them. Her mom had decorated the house and cooked favorite dishes, and there was always football on the TV.

Carrie swallowed thickly. There was no sense dwelling on painful memories. In the absence of family, a person had to make their own. Quinn and Amber were the closest thing she had, next to the Brandts. Today it didn't feel like enough, though. Something was still missing.

A strange car was parked outside the ranch house when Carrie arrived. She'd just taken her boxed pies off the seat when the front door opened and Amber came running out, her little legs churning their way down the steps toward her truck. "Carrie, Carrie! I gots to make the cranberry sauce!"

Carrie laughed and her heart warmed—and ached—as she looked down at the little girl. "I'll be sure to have an extra helping, it's my favorite," she assured Amber with a smile.

"Daddy said I couldn't help with the turkey. He said that's his job." She put on a pouty face.

"Let's see if there's something else you can help with. I'm freezing. Is it warmer inside?"

Amber took Carrie's hand without a second thought. "Yep. Duke made a big fire in the fireplace. He put on some of those green sticks and made it crackle!" Her eyes were big as silver dollars as she explained.

They started up the steps and Carrie realized Duke was standing at the top. "Happy Thanksgiving," he rumbled out, and a little zing went through her as she met his gaze.

"Happy Thanksgiving to you, too. What's this I hear about crackling fires?"

She thought he was going to reach for the pies but instead he picked up Amber and hefted her on his arm. "I put a few spruce boughs on it for fun. I've got hardwood on it now, though. Toasty warm."

Amber put her pudgy hand on his face. "I like toast."

"You like everything." He grinned at her. "Let's go in and see your dad. He and Lacey are having an argument about mashed potatoes."

Once inside the door, he put Amber down and she ran off to the kitchen. "So your sister came."

"Surprised the heck out of me. She's not the 'let's spend the holiday in the country' type."

"Apparently she is if she's here. Or maybe she just wanted to see her big brother."

He shrugged. "I doubt it. Here, let me take those while you take off your coat."

She handed him the pies and hung her coat on a hook behind the door. Stepping inside the kitchen, she heard a difference of opinion being voiced about the proper additions to mashed potatoes to make them creamy.

"Milk and butter. That's all my mother used," Quinn argued.

Carrie watched as a beautiful woman with mahogany hair leaned over the pot. "Bah. I'm telling you, you need a little sour cream and cream cheese in there. And a ricer, not a masher."

"There's a difference?"

"Oh, God." Lacey face-palmed. "You're hopeless. I'll just have to drown them in gravy."

"Is there any other way to eat mashed potatoes?"

"Well, actually…"

"Ahem," Duke interrupted, a broad grin on his face. "Lacey, you probably don't remember Carrie Coulter. She's the cattle foreman here now."

"Hi," Carrie offered shyly. Lacey Duggan was probably the most beautiful woman Carrie had ever seen— and that was saying a lot, since Kailey was drop-dead gorgeous. Lacey's long dark hair held tints of red— darker than Duke's but lustrous and thick. Her creamy skin and dark hair made the grayish-blue of her eyes incredibly striking. Carrie had felt slightly dressed up in her jeans and sweater, but Lacey's snug jeans, soft leather boots and sweater coat made Carrie feel dowdy by comparison.

"Hi," Lacey offered, smiling warmly. "My big brother says I owe my invitation to dinner to you. Nice to know he wouldn't have invited me otherwise." She raised one eyebrow at her brother.

"I gather he hasn't seen much of his family since he got home," Carrie replied, taking perverse pleasure in talking about Duke while he was standing right there. "I guess Rylan couldn't make it?"

"Rylan's somewhere in North Dakota," Duke answered. "I did call him. I said I would."

Carrie stepped forward, toward Lacey and Quinn. "I'm glad you could come. Joe always used to host, but without him this year…"

There was an awkward silence. It was clear to everyone that Quinn and Carrie had been closer to Joe than his own grandkids.

She cleared her throat. "He'd be glad you're here now. Okay, Quinn, what's left to do? How can I help?"

The uncomfortable moment passed as everyone chipped in. Quinn let Lacey have her way with the potatoes while Carrie drained the vegetables. Duke set the table and Amber was put to work putting warm buns in a basket. Quinn took Joe's good carving knife and began carving the turkey, and at the last minute Duke turned down the volume on the TV. It was showing the end of a Thanksgiving parade from somewhere, and Amber was oohing and aahing over the floats, bands and just about everything.

They were all seated at the table when Carrie looked at Duke, sitting in Joe's spot. Did he even realize that he'd taken over the head of the table? Quinn had filled the gap as best he could, but Carrie knew deep down they were all looking to Duke to take his place. As head of the ranch, head of the family. Trouble was, she knew he wasn't sure if he wanted either position.

Quinn looked at Duke. "I know I did this at the party, but I think you should give the blessing this time, Duke."

Duke's cheeks grew ruddy as he looked up. "I'm sorry, what was that?"

Lacey was looking at him strangely, and Carrie had an instant realization that Quinn was sitting on Duke's right side, and with the television running, he hadn't heard the request clearly.

"Oh, you guys and your football," Carrie chided good-naturedly. Duke's gaze met hers and she blinked. "I know the preview to the game's interesting, but we could take a few minutes to give thanks, don't you think?"

Gratitude flashed through his eyes. "Busted. If we're all ready, then..."

He gave a brief blessing for friends and family and perfect mashed potatoes and then the moment was over and there was just chatter and clanking of spoons on dishes. Quinn sat next to Amber, who was perched on a red-and-blue booster seat, and put helpings of everything on her plate, including the ruby-red cranberry sauce. The toddler chattered incessantly, filling in any gaps of conversation. Duke was quiet, but Carrie and Lacey chatted along about life in Gibson and Lacey's job in the city, working for the conservation department.

"I like to think it's important," Lacey was saying, "even though I'm not much of an outdoor girl. My talents definitely lie in pushing papers and adding columns of numbers."

"So you're not planning on taking on your third of the ranch?" Duke interjected, leaning forward a bit.

"It'll be sold after the year's up, right?"

Duke nodded, turning his attention back to his plate, but Carrie could see something was bothering him by the stiff set of his shoulders.

"Duke, are you actually thinking of staying?" Lacey put down her fork and stared at her brother. "But the army was everything to you!"

Carrie went cold. Lacey didn't know, did she? Didn't know about his injuries, his hearing, his leaving the forces. Did anyone other than her?

Lacey frowned at her brother. "I thought you were just hanging here, you know, while you were on leave or something."

"I haven't made any firm decisions," Duke answered, avoiding her gaze. "But let's enjoy dinner and put a pin in that topic for another time."

Quinn had gone quiet, too. He and Carrie both knew that their livelihoods hung in the balance if the Duggan kids didn't step up. If only Quinn could afford to buy it himself, he'd be awesome at running the place. But with his mortgage, and being a single dad... Neither one of them could afford to take any of it on. It wasn't a big ranch, but it was worth more than either of them could muster up even if they pooled their resources.

"Daddy, can I have butter for my roll, please?" Amber's voice cut into the silence.

"Of course you can," he answered, and they all went back to eating. The comfort level never quite came back, though, and Carrie felt as if she was walking on eggshells for the rest of the meal.

DUKE COULDN'T FORGET the startled look that had shadowed Carrie's face when Lacey had asked about the ranch. All the while they enjoyed their pumpkin pie and coffee, Carrie and Quinn were more subdued.

Duke hadn't expected this. He'd thought to come here and sort things out—to worry about himself and *his* future, not be burdened with everyone else's. Quinn disappeared with Amber for a while to put her down for a nap in the den and Duke felt a heavy weight descend on him. It wasn't just his future that depended on what happened here over the next several months. It was Carrie's, and Quinn's, and all the other employees who relied on their jobs at Crooked Valley.

In the army, as a platoon leader, he'd felt responsible for the men beside him. It had been a mistake to think he could leave responsibilities behind.

"Are you okay?" Lacey came up to him as he loaded plates in the dishwasher. He stole a glance over at Carrie, who was busy putting leftovers in plastic containers. "Yeah, I guess."

"You don't seem happy, Duke."

"It's nothing. I'm just trying to figure some things out." Like what to do with the ranch. Like what to do about his growing feelings for Carrie. Things were as much a mess as they'd ever been.

"You could start by unloading the ranch. You can't hide out here forever. We all know you're not the least bit serious about taking it on. Besides, I've got a job and Ry isn't the settle-in-one-spot type. Why prolong it?"

It was a weird moment to hear his grandfather's voice in his head, but he heard it just the same. *You're the eldest. It's your responsibility to look after the others. To step up, lead by example and be the head of the family.*

Grampa Joe had said that to him the day of his father's funeral, and as Duke had grown up he'd taken it pretty seriously. They'd been at cross-purposes, because Duke's interpretation of leading by example was following in his father's footsteps and joining the army, rather than taking over the family farm.

Still, as he stood in his grandparents' kitchen, he recognized the words. Accepted them. His mother had eventually remarried and built herself a new life. She'd never felt the pull of tradition and family the way Duke had. Even now, twenty-some years on, it was his job to lead by example. To be the head of the family.

To do the right thing.

"I'm not going back in the army," he said, and out of the corner of his eye he saw Carrie straighten and stare at him.

"You can't be serious. That's your career! It's all you ever wanted!" Lacey put her hands on her hips. "Why on earth would you throw that away for this? Living out in the middle of nowhere with just the horses and cattle for company?"

Carrie put the full containers in the fridge, and did it a little roughly. Did Lacey even realize she was being insulting? Carrie turned around and caught his eye and he saw the fire blazing there. In some ways Duke felt like a puppet with his grandfather pulling the strings, so it wasn't hard to imagine that she felt something similar, only Duke was the puppet master.

"If you'll excuse me, I think I'll check on the stock."

"Oh, of course!" Lacey was all smiles and Duke gritted his teeth.

"You don't have to go," he said, stepping away from the dishwasher and moving toward her. "It's your day off."

"You and your sister need some privacy to talk." She smiled, but he could tell it was forced. "Tell Quinn I've gone to the barns, will you?"

He didn't argue because he understood. A minute later and the door slammed behind her.

"That was nice of her to give us some privacy." Lacey put glasses in the dishwasher while Duke's temper simmered.

"She didn't do it to give us privacy, Lace. You don't get it, do you? Joe left this place to us. Without us there is no Crooked Valley. Without Crooked Valley, Carrie and Quinn and all the other employees are out of a job. This is their livelihood, and you were talking about it like it was a joke."

Her mouth dropped open. "Are you mad at me, Duke? Come on, you've never wanted to work this place. Or is it this Carrie woman who has you tied up in knots?"

He swallowed while the words *what if it was?* leaped unbidden into his head. "Things change," he answered, putting a serving bowl down on the counter. "I'm not going back to the army, and I need to sort out where I go from here. Turns out this isn't such a bad place to be."

"As a consolation prize? Why on earth would you

leave something you love? You're only thirty. You still have lots of healthy years!"

This was it, then—telling his family, who'd only known so far that he'd been wounded and not seriously. He had no big scars, no limps to emphasize the point. And perhaps that was what made it most difficult. It seemed terribly unfair that everything changed over an injury that was so completely invisible. It made him feel like a fraud.

"But I don't," he explained quietly. "I lost hearing in one of my ears, Lacey. And it won't ever come back. I'm half-deaf."

There was silence for a moment and then she shut the dishwasher door. "What does that mean?"

"It means my combat days are done. And that's what I loved. I don't want to be sitting behind a desk somewhere. I'd rather take a medical discharge and start over."

"Is that what Dad would have done?"

Did Lacey even remember their father? He doubted it. Duke barely remembered and he had a few years on her. "I'm not Dad," he replied. "Maybe it's time I stopped trying to be."

While his sister absorbed that revelation, he got a soap tab, reopened the dishwasher and put it in, then shut the door and hit the start button. When he turned away he realized he only heard a low hum that was the water pulsing around the dishes. It should have been louder. Clearer. How many everyday sounds was he missing out on?

Lacey put her hand on his arm. "You really can't hear?"

He stared into her eyes. His baby sister. The girl he'd lived to annoy half the time, and stood up and protected the other half. She never would have married that low-life if he'd been home to talk some sense into her. Or into him.

"Only one side," he assured her. "I turn my head a lot. Watch people's lips when they speak. I'm adjusting."

"What happened? All Mom said was that you were coming home for a while. Taking a break."

"Because that's all I told her."

"What did she say when you asked her for dinner?" He looked away. "I didn't ask."

Her next words were garbled and fuzzy, like a low murmur, and he turned his head back again. Dammit.

"What was that?" he asked, feeling stupid.

"I said you can't avoid Mom forever. I know you're not a big fan of David…"

The new husband. Duke couldn't even put his finger on why he didn't like the man. He seemed perfectly ordinary and nice. He treated Duke's mom well. She was happy. And yet he'd rather have dental work than think about spending a weekend at his mother's new house.

"It's not that…"

Lacey looked up at him, her eyes wide and a little too knowing for his comfort. "Just make sure you're not hiding yourself away here, big brother. You never wanted to be a part of the ranch, so what's changed?"

Duke thought back to the conversations he'd had with Quinn since arriving at Crooked Valley, the laughs he'd shared with the hands and the camaraderie he'd shared with all of them during the cattle drive and the resulting get-togethers. He thought of Carrie, leaving her menu closed at the diner because she had it memorized, the instant welcome he'd been given by the other ranchers at the Silver Dollar, the pinpoints of starlight late at night.

He thought of the softness of Carrie's lips as he

kissed her, the feel of her firm, toned body beneath his hands. The way she wiped her eyes in private because she'd had to show mercy to a wounded animal.

What changed was that in the absence of the life he'd known for the past twelve years, he'd made a new connection. One that would be hard to leave in the end. Crooked Valley was starting to feel like a home.

"She's got to you, hasn't she?" Lacey's voice interrupted his thoughts quietly. "Carrie. Are you in love with her?"

"It's too soon for anything like that. I like her a lot."

"Enough to settle down here? Become a rancher? Are you crazy? God, Duke, you don't know anything about raising cattle. Or horses."

Quinn returned to the kitchen, saving Duke from answering, at least for now. "Phew," Quinn said, slumping his shoulders. "I think someone had a little too much pie. Getting her to settle was an adventure today. Normally she hits the sofa in there and is out."

"Aw, she's a good kid," Duke returned. "I don't know how you do it."

"It's hard. Right now, not so bad. She's small. But once she gets older and wants all that girlie stuff? And boys?" Quinn shook his head. "She won't even remember her mother, you know? All she'll have is pictures."

Lacey looked up at Duke, then back to Quinn. "We lost our dad when we were little," she said softly. "It's hard, but Mom did a good job. You are, too. She's sweet."

Quinn's eyes lightened a little. "Thanks. It's funny what you can learn on the job when you have to." He gave a little chuckle. "Like Duke here. We might make a rancher out of him yet. If he hangs around, that is."

At that moment, Duke had an idea. He was going to

wait until after the New Year before he made any decisions. Quinn and Carrie had both been so great he knew he owed it to them to really give this a chance. It was less than six weeks. More than enough time to play with some scenarios.

And in the meantime, there was Christmas. There'd been many years he'd been stuck in barracks or overseas that he wished he could be home for a big family Christmas. Why not have one, and have it here? It had been several years since they'd all been together for Christmas, and it had been good seeing Lacey today, remembering old times.

If he could convince Rylan to come… And he'd even invite Mom and David. She might be harder to persuade. She'd always hated the ranch, and he didn't get the feeling she'd be too excited to visit. But he could extend the invite anyway.

The idea of having a real Christmas, with a tree and a few presents and the other trappings of the holidays, suddenly held a lot of attraction for Duke. If they couldn't keep the ranch in the end, maybe they could be brought closer together as a family. Maybe, he mused, that was what Joe had wanted all along. And he never would have thought of it if Carrie hadn't pressed him into inviting Lacey here today.

"I'll be here at least through Christmas," he said firmly. "I'm not going to decide anything until after the holidays. If that's okay with you, Quinn."

"I think that's great. I can use the help, and if you're around to pitch in, I'll be able to take a little more time with Amber to get ready for the holidays. Take her into the city to visit Santa and do some shopping." His eyes looked a little sad. "Marie always wanted to do that."

It was very clear to Duke that Quinn had loved his

wife deeply. It was a real tragedy that she'd been taken so young, so unfair to Quinn and Amber.

Lacey turned away and began cleaning the tablecloth and napkins off the table. "I'll just put these in the laundry," she said, her voice tight, and before Duke could answer, she disappeared down the back hall.

"Your sister's not interested in the ranch, is she?" Quinn's voice was quiet but clear, and Duke looked him in the eye.

"No, she's not," he answered. "But don't panic yet. Nothing's decided for sure, and there's time before anything will change around here. I'll make sure it's all fine, okay?"

Quinn nodded. "I think I'll go help Carrie. Four hands are better than two and she deserves a break."

A few minutes later Lacey was still in the laundry room and Quinn was walking across the yard when Carrie came out of the barn. Duke took one look at her heavy jacket and red knitted hat and felt his heart slam against his ribs.

For a man so determined to stay away from responsibilities, he was sure knee-deep in them now. Because he'd meant what he'd said to Quinn. Somehow he'd make sure that everything would work out. For everyone.

Chapter Nine

Carrie stared mindlessly at the television. While it had been great having dinner with Quinn and Duke and Lacey, once she was back home her situation became disturbingly clear.

She didn't normally mind being alone so much. She'd thought about it while she'd worked away in the barns after dinner. After her dad had vanished, she'd had her mom. And after her mom's death, she'd had Joe, who'd stood in as a father figure in so many ways. But Carrie had no one. Quinn had Amber. Duke had Lacey—and other family out there if he was willing to swallow his pride and reach out. Make an effort. How she wished she'd had a brother or sister growing up. The only thing anchoring her life right now was Crooked Valley.

And even that was up in the air. Duke was making an effort, she could see that well enough. He might even choose to stay. But unless Lacey and Rylan came through, the only home she knew was still in jeopardy.

A commercial came on the TV and she burrowed farther into her blanket, but then a swath of headlights swept across the window. With the dark outside, and the lights on inside, she couldn't see the vehicle. But the erratic beat of her heart told her she hoped it was Duke. And, oh, that was bad news.

She went to the door and peeked through the hole. Sure enough, Duke stood there, still dressed in his good jeans and his heavy jacket and Stetson, looking way sexier than she was comfortable with, carrying a bag of something in his hands.

She opened the door. "What are you doing out here?"

"Nice greeting. Makes a guy feel all warm and fuzzy."

"Sorry. Come on in." She stepped aside, feeling off balance. It had become a put-on-your-jammies-and-have-hot-cocoa night and not the optimal time to have an irresistible man show up on her doorstep. Especially a man she'd slept with. As if she could wipe *those* images from her brain...

"I brought you leftovers," he announced. "Quinn took some home with him, and I took a dish with tomorrow's lunch for me, but you didn't get anything."

"I could have gotten it tomorrow."

"But then I wouldn't be here."

She raised an eyebrow. "Yes, that's my point."

He put the bag down on the floor. "Was it that bad? Do you really want me to go?"

He was talking about their night together. She knew it and he knew it and avoiding him for a few weeks had only postponed this conversation. A conversation she was scared to have. It would be so stupid to take on a relationship knowing it was probably temporary. And a very good way for her to get hurt.

"I don't know what to say, Duke."

"Try the truth."

But the truth was the most difficult thing of all, making her vulnerable. "The truth is it's easier to put things in perspective when you're not around. When you're standing right in front of me, logic flies right out the window."

He chuckled. "I'm flattered."

She turned away. "It's not a compliment."

He laughed again. "That's why I'm flattered."

"You're impossible!"

He took off his boots and left them at the door, then picked up the bag. "You should put this stuff in the fridge."

Exasperating, that was what he was. Carrie snatched the bag from his hand and took it to the kitchen, plunking it down on the counter.

"Easy," he said, his socked feet soundless on the floor. "There's pie in there."

She took out plastic dishes of turkey and stuffing, mashed potatoes, peas and pie, and would have put them all in the fridge except he stayed her hand with his fingers. "Leave the pie. I've got a hankering for another piece."

"I don't remember asking you in for pie," she pointed out, wondering why she was being so snippy when she'd just been sitting here feeling alone and isolated. Now she had company and she was being rude.

"Miss Coulter, might I join you in a piece of this delicious pumpkin pie?" he asked, a twinkle in his eye and his voice as sweet and smooth as buckwheat honey. He looked so entreating that she couldn't resist, and a smile crept across her lips.

"You're incorrigible."

"So I've been told."

She put the other dishes in the fridge and returned, taking two forks out of a drawer. "Let me get a few plates," she said, reaching for a cupboard handle.

"We don't need plates." He popped open the dish. "Here."

He rested his hips against the counter and plunged his fork into the pie. Fascinated, she watched as he lifted the fork to his lips and popped the morsel into his mouth. "Aren't you going to join me?" he asked, holding out the dish.

She hesitated.

"Come on," he cajoled. "It's so good. Creamy and rich and spicy, just the way I like it."

Her cheeks flamed. That had been deliberate. He was trying to provoke her and it was working.

She took a small piece on her fork and ate it. "There, satisfied?" she asked.

He met her gaze. "Not even close."

He put more pie on his fork and held it out for her to taste. "Come on, Carrie," he urged, his voice low. "It's delicious."

"You're trying to seduce me with pie," she said, embarrassed that it was actually working. Pumpkin pie and flannel pajamas. Not exactly your typical sexy trappings for a seduction scene.

Duke put down the fork. "Truth?" he asked, his gaze steady on hers. "I don't want to stay away from you any longer. I understand why you took a step back. Things got a little intense. I know you're concerned about what the men might think and how that might affect your authority. I'm not oblivious, Carrie. But I'm tired of pretending I don't want to be with you when I do."

Her breath came out in a rush. This was definitely worse than the pie....

"I know nothing is settled. I don't know what's going to happen with Crooked Valley and I can't—I won't—make promises that I don't know if I can keep. I don't

know what the future holds, and if we take this anywhere at all we both need to accept that going in."

"You really think it'll be easy to walk away when
the time comes? I'm not naive, Duke. I know there's a
good chance you'll be going again, and where will that
leave me? I'm not sure how resilient I am. I'm not the
kind of girl who can engage in a torrid affair without
feelings involved."

He put the dish down on the counter. "Are you saying you're in love with me, Carrie?"

"God, no." It was far too soon to even consider such
a thing. "But I'm not lying to myself, either. If we carry
on the way we started, it won't be a breeze to shake
hands and say good luck in the end."

"So you'd rather stop it in its tracks. Avoid that type
of situation altogether."

She nodded.

He took two steps forward, until he was standing directly in front of her. To her surprise he reached out and
took her hands in his. "Part of what the military taught
me was that there are never any guarantees. Never any
absolutes. Maybe I'm leaving again, maybe I'm not. We
never know if we're going to be here tomorrow or next
month or next year, but we can't stop living because of
it." He squeezed her fingers. "I don't know how this will
end, but I know I want to be with you. Spend time with
you. I feel better when you're around. Not to mention
the crazy chemistry we have going on."

Chemistry indeed. It had zinged between them from
that very first dance at the saloon, refusing to be ignored.

"I'm here until the New Year at least," he said quietly. "We can be discreet."

"A secret," she answered, her brows pulling together a bit.

"No, not a secret. That makes it sound like we're ashamed." He gazed into her eyes. "I'm not. We're adults. We don't need to sneak around. I just mean... maybe we can hold on to our privacy. What we do is our business."

It was the oddest proposition she'd ever received, and yet it was the most heartfelt, too. He wasn't making pretty promises; he was being completely honest. She wasn't into taking chances with her heart, but something he said struck a chord, too. What was she going to do, lock herself away in this house waiting for a guarantee that she wouldn't get hurt? That didn't make any sense, either.

But this was a different sort of choice. This was deliberately moving forward knowing perfectly well that the odds were it wouldn't last. Could she take the leap and just commit herself to enjoying a month of Duke and then walking away?

He let go of one of her hands and lifted his, tucking a piece of hair behind her ear. "I came out here tonight because I was sitting alone and I knew you were sitting alone and it didn't make any sense when we like being together." He kissed her softly, his mouth tugging slightly on her lips, making her knees wobble a little bit. "I can't stop thinking about kissing you. About making love to you. I can't stand the idea that our one time was our last time. That's why I'm here, Carrie. I'm not ready to give up yet. And I had to know if you felt the same."

This was the moment where she could say no and end it right here. The future was in front of her, and all she could see was a blurry gray area with no focus. What was crystal clear, though, was the next several weeks.

She could say no and face days of the same empty house over and over, of a few evenings at the bar with Kailey doing exactly the same thing, of an empty holiday with sympathy invitations for poor single Carrie. Or she could put her hand in Duke's and they could navigate these few weeks together. She could let the future take care of itself—it always did in the end, as she well knew.

"I don't want to get hurt," she murmured, lifting her eyes to his.

"And I'll do my best not to hurt you. Can't we just take it one day at a time? Not worry about the future?"

She swallowed. His fingers were rubbing over her knuckles and she knew there was only one answer she could give. The one she truly wanted to give, and all that was holding her back was fear.

Her fingers clasped his tightly and, with her heart pounding, she tugged his hand and began the short walk down the hall to her bedroom. Once inside, she shut the door behind them, enclosing them in the intimate space, the centerpiece of the room being the double bed.

"You're sure?" he asked quietly.

"I'm not the kind to have affairs. To think about the here and now and not the future. Maybe I need to learn how to do more of that." She looked up at him and found a little more confidence. "When you lose the people you love, you sometimes forget to keep living. You think you're protecting yourself from getting hurt again. But maybe you miss out on a lot of good things, too. I think I need some good things in my life. I think I need you, Duke. For however long I can have you."

"I think I need you, too," he replied, grazing his thumb over her cheek. "Let's just take it as it comes. If either of us needs to back off at any time…no hard feelings."

He made it sound so logical. Could it really be that simple?

"No hard feelings," she echoed. And whatever misgivings that remained were forgotten as he reached for her.

BLACK FRIDAY DIDN'T actually dawn. The sky turned marginally lighter as big flakes of snow fluttered to the ground, building up on the corners of Carrie's bedroom window. Carrie blinked and rolled slightly, staring at the curve of Duke's shoulder. Lord, he was beautiful. And strong. And way too charismatic for her good.

She wasn't sure at all about this new arrangement they had going—she had a sneaky suspicion that it would leave her hurt in the end. And yet...there was a warm glow inside her that she knew was down to Duke and his attention. He made her feel beautiful, desirable, wanted. It was something very new. She had never considered herself much of a girlie girl, but Duke made her feel...womanly.

She giggled a little, amazed at even having those thoughts. What in the world had come over her?

Duke stirred and rolled over, his eyes slowly opening. "Well. I guess I slept over."

"I guess you did," she answered, secretly pleased that he hadn't felt the need to get up and leave in the middle of the night. Waking up beside him was kind of special, and a first for her.

Five weeks, she reminded herself. *In five weeks he could be gone. For once, just enjoy it, girl.*

"Is it snowing?"

"It looks that way." She snuggled closer to him since her heat hadn't kicked in. "We should get back to the ranch. But you're so nice and warm...."

His arms came around her. "It's freezing in here. Your nose is like ice."

She had the thermostat set to go down at night to save on heating bills. "I like warm covers and cool air for sleeping," she answered. "I'll go turn up the heat."

The floor was cold on her feet and she zipped out to the hall, turned up the main thermostat and ran back to bed, jumping back under the covers. "I think the temp really dropped last night."

"Do you think everything is okay at home?" Duke raised up on an elbow.

"It's just a regular snowfall. The stock will be fine." She grinned, secretly pleased that he'd referred to the ranch as *home*. "Are you worried about them?"

"Maybe a little."

"That's good. It shows you care." She rolled over to her back. "You know, Quinn and the boys will have things under control. It would be a good day for me to show you some of the records, and I've got some decisions to make for next spring and what we're going to seed. It's a delicate balance, caring for the longevity of the land and trying to produce the best beef possible."

"I'm learning there's a lot of science to ranching. It's not just feeding animals and then selling them off."

"Joe always said he wanted the ranch land to still be rich and fertile hundreds of years from now, so it could support and sustain."

"Like a caretaker."

Carrie's heart warmed. "Yes, like that. We call it stewardship. Taking care of the land that takes care of us. Quinn's the main boss when it comes to all this, and we talk a lot about what I want to do to keep the cattle side as profitable as possible while maintaining the integrity of the land and the overall goals at the same time. I know we're employees, Duke, but we care. We really do."

"I know that. Joe was very lucky to have you."

"He taught us and then he trusted us. He would have done the same for you."

Duke's body tensed slightly and he pulled away. Not much, but enough that she felt the withdrawal.

"Sorry," she apologized softly. "I know you don't like to talk about him."

"It's okay. Look, when I got here I was a little angry that in the end Joe got his way—he got me on the ranch just like he always wanted. I'm not so angry about that now."

"That's good, isn't it?"

"In some ways." He brushed a piece of hair off her face. "I'm certainly not sorry I met you."

She got that delicious, weightless feeling in her stomach again.

His face sobered. "But I have regrets, too. I was selfish, Carrie. I was so bent on making my point that I overlooked the fact that he loved this place. I wish I'd made more of an effort to see him over the years. I can't fix that."

"And you like to fix things, don't you?"

"I don't know. Maybe."

She smiled and rolled to face him. "Oh, you do. It goes right back to the day you earned your nickname. Know what I think? I think you had to make a choice, and you followed in your dad's footsteps because buckling to the pressure to be involved in the ranch would seem like a betrayal to his memory. To your duty as his son."

Duke sat up, the bedspread pooling around his hips.

"Damn, Carrie." He slid out of bed and pulled on his jeans. "I didn't stay over so I could be psychoanalyzed."

"That wasn't my intention."

He spun around, agitation marring his face. "Could you repeat that? I didn't hear you."

How easily she forgot about his hearing problem. On the outside Duke appeared perfect. But he had scars. Physical and emotional. Regrets were like that. She should know.

"I said," she repeated, well aware of his attention to her lips, "that I didn't mean to go all shrink on you. I just meant that you should give yourself a break. You can't be all things to everyone, Duke."

He sat back down on the edge of the bed and sighed. "It's an underdog thing," he admitted. "I might have liked my time here more when I was a kid. I know my dad did, even if he did choose the forces over farming. It's just that…I heard so often that if he'd only stayed home and not gone into the army, he would still be around. Like he'd let them down or failed them somehow. For God's sake, he *died*. That should have been sacrifice enough."

And he'd rushed to defend his dad by following his example. Oh, what a loyal and tender heart he had underneath the steely strength. "Your dad would be proud of you. And I think Joe would, too. If he didn't believe in you, he would have set things up differently. I think he understood more than you realize."

In a way, it hurt her just a bit that Joe hadn't told her—or Quinn—his plans in his will. They'd given the ranch years of dedication. They'd been more than employees. They'd been like family. Duke wasn't the only one to feel a bit manipulated.

"Anyway," she said, changing the subject to something lighter. "Let's get some breakfast and head over. I'll give you a tutorial on grassland management."

They got up and dressed, and Carrie quickly scrambled some eggs and made toast while Duke shoveled off the steps. When he stomped his way back in, he was frowning. "It's really coming down. Not a blizzard, but a good snowfall. The roads are gonna be slick."

She scooped eggs onto a plate and handed it to him, then reached into the fridge for jam. "I wonder if it's just our elevation or if it's more widespread. It'll put a damper on all the Black Friday sales." She laughed. "Not that I care. I like a good bargain as much as the next guy, but my idea of fun isn't cramming myself into a store full of crazy people."

"What is your idea of fun?"

She took her plate to the table. "I dunno. I guess a hot cup of coffee while watching the snow is a good start. Going for a ride at sunset. Fishing in the creek and making a snowman."

"You really are an outdoor girl, aren't you?"

She nodded. "Yup. Though I'm also partial to chick flicks and chocolate-covered raisins. I like to keep it simple."

"I like that about you."

Their eyes met, and she quickly looked down at her toast. She could get too used to this. Chemistry, yes, but she liked him. Liked him a lot.

Just enjoy it, the voice inside repeated to her.

After breakfast Carrie quickly washed the dishes and put them in the drying rack. Duke stared out the window, and when she was ready to go, she put her hand on his arm. "We should get going," she said.

"You might want to throw a few things in a bag," he suggested, his face grim. "It looks bad, and we can go in my truck. I'll bring you home tomorrow, when the roads are better. Or you can take the day off...."

"I took the day off yesterday for the holiday, and there's still stuff to be done." She frowned.

"Listen, if you don't want to stay with me, stay at the house. No obligation. I just don't want you driving back down here tonight. If the weather clears, I'll bring you back. I just think you should be prepared."

"All right, all right." She went to her room and threw a change of clothes and a basic bag of toiletries into a backpack. She'd driven between the ranch and home lots of times in bad weather and been fine. But then, Joe and Eileen had put her up lots of times, too. How was this different?

The answer to that was painfully obvious. One snow-storm and lines were already being blurred.

Chapter Ten

Quinn was already at the house when they arrived, a full pot of coffee brewed and a bag of day-old pastries on the counter. He raised an eyebrow when Carrie and Duke showed up together, but Carrie kept her cool and merely remarked, "Duke gave me a ride today in the storm."

Whether or not Quinn believed her didn't matter. He went about his business, sitting at the kitchen table with a laptop while Amber sat opposite him, coloring with broad scribbles in a coloring book.

"Hey sweetie," Carrie said, kissing Amber's blond head. It smelled like strawberry shampoo. "Whatcha coloring?"

"Flowers," she answered, scribbling inside a patch of what appeared to be daisies.

"Pretty."

"I brought her with me rather than drive all the way into town for day care. The roads looked slippery."

"They were," Duke said, handing Carrie a coffee fixed the way she liked. Carrie saw Quinn's gaze on the coffee cup and she felt exposed all over again. Or perhaps he wasn't thinking anything at all and she was just feeling guilty?

"I thought I'd give Duke a rundown on the plans for

next year's pasture management," Carrie said. "Unless there's something else you need done with the stock."

"The boys were here first thing this morning and looked after things. I sent them home again. I figured Duke and I could handle what needed doing this afternoon."

"Sure," Duke answered.

"Want cookies," Amber announced.

Quinn sighed. "Maybe later, okay, munchkin? How about some cartoons?"

She picked up another crayon. "Then cookies?"

"We'll see, okay?"

Carrie and Duke made their way to the office, where Carrie booted up the main computer and turned on the space heater. The snow was really piling up, and the coffee was hot and strong. "I know it can be a pain in the behind, but I love the snow. Especially the fluffy, big flakes like right now. It's kind of magical, don't you think?"

"There were a lot of years I didn't get to see snow," Duke revealed. "A lot of years I wasn't home for holidays. I enjoyed yesterday. I think I'm going to enjoy being back in Montana for Christmas, too."

She put in her password and waited while everything loaded. "Do you have plans?"

"Actually, I got thinking after yesterday's dinner. It was nice having Lacey here." He pulled up a spare chair on casters and rolled his way to the side of the desk. "What do you think about having Christmas here, at the ranch? Would that be okay?"

It sounded so perfect that it was scary. "It's your ranch," she said quietly. "You don't have to run it past me."

He put his hand on her arm. "It's been more your

home than mine, Carrie. I want to ask Lacey, and Rylan, and my mom and her new husband, and Quinn and Amber and you. I want to get a big tree and have presents and the whole nine yards. Do you know how long it's been since I had a Christmas like that?"

She swallowed against the lump in her throat. There was such yearning in his voice, whether he knew it or not. She suspected the last time he had a big family Christmas was probably right around the time she'd had one, too.

When her mother and father had been together, and it had been the three of them. Christmas morning had been quiet as an only child, but happy. And they'd always made a big breakfast and gone to church and then Carrie's mom had cooked a dinner, divided portions into tin plates with lids and delivered them to less-fortunate people who didn't have family to share the holiday with. People who had been forgotten or left behind.

She blinked against the tears that had formed in her eyes, and to her chagrin a few slipped over her lashes and down her cheeks.

"Hey," Duke said softly, pushing his chair closer to hers and putting his hands on her knees. "I didn't mean to upset you. We don't have to do it. It was just an idea."

She sniffled. "I think it's a great idea. I just got sentimental, that's all." She wiped her lashes and let out a shaky breath. "My mom loved Christmas. She decorated and baked and we delivered Christmas dinners to seniors and shut-ins. But that all changed when she got sick. I haven't had a good Christmas like that in so long. Joe always included me, but it was quiet and I think he always thought of the people who were missing."

"I should have been here...."

"Life is too short for shoulds. I think Joe and Eileen

would be happy that you want to do this. And your family, too. Whatever help you need, let me know."

"You might be sorry you said that."

"Maybe." She smiled through her tears. Truthfully, she tended to dread the holidays. She usually volunteered to look after the chores so the other employees could spend the day with their families. As she'd said, Joe and Eileen included her, but it hadn't been the same. Since her mother's death two years ago, she hadn't even bothered with a tree at the house.

But first there was work to do. "Let's get started on this first," she suggested, opening up a program. "I'll show you what we did last year, explain why we did it and our long-term plans. Then I'll start putting together a plan for this year. Once that's complete—not today, of course—I'll take it to Quinn and we'll go over it, make changes. In the spring we might tweak it again, after we do some soil testing."

They got to work and the Christmas talk was forgotten, but only temporarily. Quinn came in later to say he was going to check on one of the horses that had a quarter crack and would they mind watching Amber for a little while. She offered to go instead of Quinn, but to her surprise Duke said he'd stay with Amber if two sets of hands would be better than one.

"You're sure?" Quinn asked. "She can be a handful."

"We'll be fine. I'll have her reading and doing algebra before you get back." Duke grinned in the disarming way he could and Quinn laughed.

"Okay," he agreed, his tone implying, "You asked for it."

Carrie and Quinn bundled up and trudged their way to the horse barn. She and Quinn examined the hoof and then checked on the other equine stock before heading back to the house. The snow still fell, the flakes smaller and harder now as they drifted along the sides of the path.

They were stamping their boots as they entered the house, and a delicious smell wafted from the kitchen to the foyer. It was followed by a gleeful giggle and clapping of hands.

"What's going on in here?" Carrie and Quinn walked into the kitchen and halted straightaway. The butcher block was covered in flour. Amber was standing on a dining chair and Duke had pinned a dish towel on her as a makeshift apron. She had flour on the tip of her nose and down one cheek, plus a smudge on her pink-and-purple top. Duke, to Carrie's shock, was wrist-deep in some sort of dough, a gigantic grin on his face.

"We're makin' cookies!" Amber's delighted voice piped up through the silence.

Quinn raised an eyebrow. "You are full of surprises, Duke."

He laughed and kneaded the dough a little more. "I still have one or two up my sleeve. When a guy's single, and likes cookies, he learns how."

"You haven't heard of a grocery store?" Carrie laughed. Amber was fairly hopping from one foot to the other, eager to get her hands messy.

"What's the fun in that?" he asked. He took his hands out of the bowl. Dough clung to his long fingers. "Okay, put your hands in and squeeze it around a bit. When it gets good and soft, we'll make it into a ball and you can roll it out with the rolling pin."

With her tongue between her teeth, Amber started working the dough with her small fingers. After a few moments, Duke put his in the bowl, too, and the two of them laughed as they formed the buttery dough into a smooth ball.

"My fingers are dirty," Amber announced, holding up her hands.

"Hmm, mine, too," Duke answered. With an impish smile, he lifted his hand and began licking the dough off his fingers.

Amber giggled, Duke waggled his eyebrows and Carrie began the precarious fall into love.

Duke had taken Amber to the sink to wash her hands when the timer on the oven dinged. "Do you think you could take out the pan that's in there?" he asked Carrie, looking over his shoulder.

So that was what the smell was. Not the cookie dough, but a pan of mystery squares that were brown and spicy-looking. Carrie took a pot holder and lifted them out of the oven, putting them on top of the glass top stove. "I can't believe you had the ingredients for this," she said, putting down the pot holder and inhaling the rich scent.

"Joe had a pretty well-stocked cupboard. I noticed the groceries when I was working around yesterday, getting dinner." Duke spread flour on the butcher block in preparation for the dough. "It seems strange, this house being empty. It's like it's half lived in and half vacant, you know?"

Quinn looked up from his laptop. "You could always move back in."

But Duke shook his head. "Naw, it's not for me. This house needs something more." Carrie watched his gaze move to Amber. "Like a family." He took a moment to show Amber how to sprinkle the dough with flour and let her start rolling it out. "You know, there's no reason why you couldn't move in here, Quinn. It'd save you the drive and you'd be on-site."

Carrie had thought the same thing in the weeks since Joe's sudden death, but hadn't brought it up. It wasn't her house to offer.

"Thanks, but I like to keep things as stable as possible. With the future of the ranch undecided, I don't want to move Amber and then have to maybe move again."

Carrie watched as Duke smoothed out some of Amber's dough and sent her for the cookie sheet. "Keeping things familiar for her is probably pretty important."

Quinn agreed.

Amber pulled on Duke's sleeve. "Can we cut them out now?"

Carrie stepped forward. "Can I help? I love making cookies."

Amber beamed. "Yes, yes! You can help, Carrie!"

Carrie looked up at Duke. She'd seen him dressed in all sorts of ways, but right now, in jeans and a shirt with flour and little bits of dough stuck on his hands, he was irresistible. She was starting to see depths to him she hadn't even imagined existed. Depths that showed what a wonderful man he could be.

"It seems we don't have any cookie cutters," she mentioned, wishing her words didn't sound quite so breathy.

"I don't expect they were high on Joe's list of baking priorities," Duke answered, his gaze meeting hers. "But I thought this would work." He held up a tiny juice glass. "The perfect size for shortbreads."

Amber was looking up at him as if he hung the moon and stars. Carrie wondered if she gazed at him the same way.

"You girls can cut out the cookies, and I'll cut the squares. We're going to do something fun with them."

As Carrie helped Amber cut out the cookies with the

small tumbler, Duke took a knife and cut the squares into small cubes. The first pan of cookies went in and the timer was set, and then they went to work rolling the cubes of warm, spicy squares into balls while Amber rolled them in sugar and put them in an empty ice-cream container Duke had unearthed from a cupboard somewhere.

"Try one," he suggested, and Carrie popped one into her mouth. It was a little like gingerbread, a little like cookies, soft and chewy.

"Those are delicious."

Amber chewed on one thoughtfully. "I like chocklit."

They both laughed. "My mom used to make these around the holidays," he said. "I called her and asked for the recipe. She didn't even have to look it up. Knew it by heart."

He'd called his mom. Something inside her expanded, warm and happy. He was reaching out to his family, settling in here. Dare she hope that he'd hang around longer than just for the holidays?

"I invited her for Christmas. Just put it out there for her to think about," he added. "I'm not sure if they'll come or not. But I'm hoping they will."

"I'm glad," she murmured, sneaking another ball and popping it into her mouth.

The first sheet of cookies came out and a second went into the oven. Amber was getting restless, so while Quinn kept working, they set her up at the table with two shortbread cookies and a glass of milk.

"I suppose now I get to clean up this mess."

"I'll help. We can go over more of the cattle records after if you like."

They ran water in the sink, put baking supplies away

in the sparsely filled cupboard. "You went through a lot of Joe's supplies."

He nodded. "I never really thought about it before. How he was just…here. Then gone. It must have been hard on you."

She swallowed. "It was. I still miss him. It isn't the same without him here. Quinn and I know what we're doing, but it felt different when he was alive, having him at the helm."

"He was a good boss, then."

"He was a leader." She grabbed a dish towel. "Quinn's a great manager. I can handle the cattle. But what we're missing is leadership."

Leadership that Duke could provide. It wasn't all about knowing everything there was to know about ranching. It was bigger than that. It was being someone who could be trusted, who listened, who inspired confidence. Duke, whether he knew it or not, had all those traits. He was more like his grandfather than he probably cared to admit.

After the dishes were done, they retreated to the office again. They'd worked for a long time sorting through livestock records when Carrie looked out the window and started laughing.

The snow had let up a little, and Quinn and Amber had put on their gear and were outside attempting to build a snowman. So far Quinn had built an enormous bottom ball and was trying to get the second ball up on top of the first, only it wasn't budging. Amber's little hands were on the side of the huge orb, completely ineffectual.

Carrie looked over at Duke. "When was the last time you built a snowman?"

A grin climbed his cheek. "I don't know. When I was about eight?"

"There might be some carrots leftover from dinner yesterday," she suggested.

"You want to go out there?"

"Come on," she said, clicking off the monitor. "You took a cookie break. Why not take a snowman break?"

"You did say you liked building snowmen."

They bundled up quickly, pausing to grab a scarf from the closet and a large carrot from the fridge. Outside, the snow fell lightly, as though the weather was taking a breath from the hard work of dumping white stuff for hours. Amber's nose was cherry-red and her eyes danced as Carrie and Duke joined them on the front lawn.

Together the four of them hefted the middle snowball on top of the first, and Carrie went around the "seam" between the two layers and packed in reinforcing snow. Amber started rolling the ball for the head while her dad helped her, and Duke jogged off to the brush and shrubs along the edge of the driveway. By the time the ball was done, he was back with two forked sticks. They lifted the head onto the top, packed it in tight and then Duke stuck in the branches for arms. Quinn put the nose on, Carrie used two rocks for eyes and Amber looped the scarf around the snowman's neck, reaching around the huge white mass while being held by her father's strong arms.

They stood back and admired their handiwork.

Amber leaned over and whispered something in her dad's ear.

"You should tell Duke," Quinn nodded solemnly.

She turned her pixie face to Carrie and Duke. "We should name him Joe," Amber said.

Carrie looked over at Duke. Did he appreciate all the reminders of his grandfather, or did he feel overshadowed by them? They all spoke of Joe as if he was the be-all and end-all. But Duke just smiled at Amber. "I think that's a great idea," he answered.

Carrie was starting to understand that the little girl was wrapping Duke clear around her little finger.

Amber leaned over to her dad and whispered something else, and Quinn laughed.

"What now?"

Quinn didn't answer. He just put Amber down, reached for a handful of snow, quickly formed it into a ball and let it fly at Duke, hitting him square in the chest. Amber collapsed in the snow in a fit of giggles while a foolish look spread across Duke's face.

He bent and scooped up some snow and sent his snowball in Quinn's direction, but Quinn darted to the side and Duke missed. The sound of Quinn's dry laugh echoed through the yard, making Carrie smile. Cautiously, she took a few steps sideways, putting some distance between her and Duke. She wouldn't put it past him to use her as a human shield....

While Amber giggled and Quinn and Duke sent a few snowballs back and forth, Carrie stealthily made her way to a pine tree about twenty feet away. Hiding behind the trunk, she made a good half-dozen snowballs before Duke noticed she was missing.

"Hey, where'd Carrie go?"

She waited until he was looking in another direction before stepping out from behind the tree and nailing him with a snowball.

"Ow!" The snowball exploded as it connected with his shoulder.

She reached for another as the sound of Quinn's

mocking laughter reached her ears, and Amber jumped up, shouting, "Get him, Carrie!"

A ball popped against the trunk of the tree—a dead hit if she hadn't moved behind the trunk again. The white circle of snow stuck to the bark, a warning that the next time she might not be so lucky. She adjusted the weight of the snowball in her hand, darted out from behind the tree on the opposite side and let another one rip. It just glanced off his leg, and he took a menacing step forward, then another. Quinn attempted a distraction by hitting Duke on the arm, but Duke was undeterred. He'd locked on to his objective and he was determined to take it.

She grabbed another ball and fired it in his direction, then grabbed the other three she'd made and dashed across the yard, looking for another position. The only cover was the snowman they'd just made, but it was huge and solid and the perfect hostage.

She ran behind it, dropped two snowballs while weighing another in her hand. "Stop right there, Duggan, or the snowman gets it!"

"No!" Amber cried out from her spot nearby. Carrie looked over at the girl and gave a broad wink to reassure her. But it had been enough for Duke to pause, and Carrie nailed him with her next snowball, immediately dropping to reach for another.

She was all teed up and ready to let another one fly when a snowball thwacked against her back. She turned to see Quinn with one eyebrow raised, his eyes twinkling. "I would have sided with you," he said, "until you brought the snowman into it. I can't let you hurt an innocent bystander."

"Yay, Daddy!" Amber jumped up and down. She made her own snowball, sent it in Carrie's direction. It hit the mark, surprisingly, a light poof of contact. Carrie dutifully called out, "Ouch!"

The distraction was all Duke had needed. When she spun back, he was running in her direction, charging the enemy. She couldn't get her arm back fast enough and he football-tackled her, sending her into the cushy snow.

Her breath whooshed out of her lungs and she took a deep breath in and started to laugh. "No fair!" she protested. "That was three against one!"

"All's fair in love and war," Duke announced, pushing her shoulders down into the snow and then straddling her so she couldn't get up. "Shame on you for taking a hostage. That's playing dirty, Coulter, and now you've got to pay the price."

Oh, God. He was sitting on her and laughing at her and his threat filled her with delicious anticipation. What was he going to do?

"You're bluffing." She grinned up at him, taunting. "You're just a big bluffy bluffer."

"Oh, yeah?"

And he picked up a handful of snow and proceeded to wash her face with it.

Cold snow trickled down the neck of her jacket and was icy-hot against the skin of her cheeks. She sputtered and spit out the bits that had gotten into her mouth, turning her head from side to side.

His face was close to hers as he whispered, "Bluffy bluffer, huh?"

"I'm gonna make you pay," she promised in an undertone. "Later."

"I'm counting on it." His gaze met hers. There was something there, something amazing and awesome that made her heart thump against her ribs. It was more than chemistry, more than physical attraction—although they clearly had that in abundance. She liked Duke. The chip he'd had on his shoulder when he'd arrived was slowly eroding away and the man beneath it was funny, generous, warm.

No matter what happened, she was going to hold on to this time together. She felt happy. Not just content— but happy. It had been a long time since she'd had that feeling and she would enjoy it for as long as it lasted.

He slid off her and hopped up, holding out a hand. "Truce?"

She laughed, took his hand, and he pulled her to his feet. "I'm not sure how much of a truce it is. It feels more like surrender to me."

Their gazes locked again until she heard Quinn coughing discreetly.

"Right." She shook herself away from Duke's seductive gaze and smiled at Amber and Quinn. "Who wants hot chocolate?"

Chapter Eleven

The next two weeks passed in a blur for Duke. He learned a lot about ranching that he'd never considered before, and spent chilly days on horseback checking on fence lines, the health of the herd, the status of the feed stacks strategically placed in the pastures. He spent time with Carrie. It would have been easy to fall into a pattern of spending each night with her, but he held back. Truth was, despite all his learning and working, he still wasn't sure what he was going to do. The decision wasn't a light one. If he chose to stay here, it was a big commitment. A life commitment. He didn't want to get himself in too deep only to change his mind and leave again.

The first Saturday of December was crisp and sunny, a perfect winter's day. Duke hadn't done any holiday shopping and the only decorations he'd managed were whatever he'd found in the attic of the farmhouse—which wasn't much. There were tree decorations and some table linens, but the outdoor lights were a tangled ball of wire and bulbs, and when Duke plugged them in, nothing happened. He'd have to try each bulb to see if it worked—and the sets looked old enough he wasn't sure the problem was the bulbs anyway.

Carrie was coming across the yard, dressed in her

boots and heavy jacket and warmest knitted hat. She was some woman. Smart, hardworking, strong…and yet at times the most alluring, beautiful, sexy woman he'd ever known. She kept him on his toes and then some. The fact that she didn't pressure him into making any decisions made him grateful. He was a very lucky man at this moment.

He stepped out on the bunkhouse porch. "Hey, Coulter!"

She turned her head toward him and a grin lit up her face. She changed direction and headed back his way.

"Good morning," she offered, stamping her boots on the veranda floor. "You got coffee on? I could use a cup."

"Of course I do. Come on in."

He stood aside as she entered. She'd been here often enough now that she took off her coat and hung it on a hook, took off her boots and made her way right to the kitchen, grabbed herself a mug and made a beeline for the coffeemaker.

He liked having her here, and that was a little bit disturbing. He'd always had to share space or lived in cramped quarters with others. Having his own house felt like a luxury. Usually he tried to keep his space his own, but he didn't seem to mind sharing it with Carrie.

"So what's on the agenda for today?" she asked, taking her first sip.

"I thought I'd take a run into Great Falls. I need to do some Christmas shopping, and grab some lights and stuff."

"You're decorating?"

"I'm going to try, but I'm pretty out of practice. You want to come along?"

She frowned into her cup. "Shopping? On a Saturday in December? Are you insane?"

Rats. "Hey, you did say if I needed any help…"

She gave him a nasty look.

"You must be the only woman alive who doesn't like shopping."

She shrugged. "Hey, I like it fine. When I have a list, and I go on maybe a Tuesday morning when the crowds are smaller. Get in, get it done, get out."

He laughed. It was his philosophy, too. And if he'd thought of it, he would have gone earlier in the week for just that reason.

"So you're going to make me go alone? I have no idea what to buy. I haven't bought Christmas decorations in years."

"Lights. Tinsel. A wreath for the door. It's not rocket science."

Oh, she was really putting up a fight. And he'd been prepared to go by himself. Now that she was here, and clearly not enamored of the idea of shopping, he really wanted her to go with him. "I'm a guy. I won't get the right thing."

Her lips twitched.

"I'll throw in lunch. Come on, Carrie. Put on some good jeans, go into town with me. Misery loves company."

She took another sip of her coffee.

"It's for the greater good. The big Duggan family Christmas, remember? Besides, I want to pick out something for Amber and I have no idea what to buy for little girls."

Amber had them both wrapped around her finger. He could see Carrie softening, and went in for the kill.

"Besides," he added softly, "it feels like I've hardly seen you this week."

Bingo. She let out a big sigh. "All right, you win. But I need to go home and change out of barn clothes."

He waited while she changed, and they headed into Great Falls and the mall. It made the most sense to hit the department store so they could get everything they needed at once. Carrie held the list they'd made during the drive. This wasn't just a shopping expedition. It was a mission.

Carrie hadn't been joking. She didn't mess around. They hit the seasonal decor section first, loading up on outdoor lights, a wreath and hanger for the front door, and an absurd number of large red bows, which she insisted were necessary. He added a Christmas tree skirt he liked as well as new lights for the tree. The less he had to untangle and sort out, the better.

After that, she helped him choose presents for his mother, Lacey and Rylan, and he grabbed a new pair of heavy, warm work gloves for Quinn. For Amber, she told him that he couldn't go wrong with a stuffed animal and the cuter the better. After more deliberation than he cared to admit, he chose a soft brown bear with big black eyes and a red-and-green plaid ribbon around his neck. It was nearly as big as Amber. He put it in the cart and avoided looking at Carrie. He had a soft spot for the little girl, and he knew if he looked at Carrie, it would be written all over his face.

By the time they loaded their loot in the backseat of his truck, his stomach was growling. "Where do you want to go for lunch?" he asked.

"Wherever. I'm easy to please."

"I'm starting to realize that." He cranked up the

heater and looked over at her. "You're very low maintenance, Carrie. Why is that?"

She shrugged. "I don't know. I've always just kept things simple, that's all."

He thought for a few moments. From the look of her house, and the fact that her dad had left them and her mom had been so ill, he was sure part of it had to do with the fact that she couldn't afford to be high maintenance. And reading between the lines, he'd also guess that she tended to look after others rather than splurge on herself. They were wonderful qualities, ones he appreciated and respected. But it made him wonder when someone had spoiled her last. He couldn't picture it. He wondered if she even remembered what it was like to be spoiled.

He wasn't exactly rolling in cash either, but he was doing okay. He reached over across the seat and took her hand. He wanted to do something special for her. Something indulgent and nice—something that put her first.

"There's a diner just before you hit the highway," she suggested. "It shouldn't be as busy, and the food's good. A lot of truckers stop there."

He chuckled. "You know, I'd take you out for a nice lunch. It doesn't have to be a truck stop. The kind with cloth napkins and stuff."

She smiled at him. "That's a nice thought. But really? I'd love a bacon cheeseburger and chocolate milkshake, and you won't find any better than at this place. It's on the way and it won't break the bank. Perfect, right?"

So money *was* an issue with her. He wondered if he was paying her enough and felt guilty for not checking before. He didn't even know what the industry standard was, for Pete's sake. He'd learned a lot, but gosh. There was still so much more. Maybe they'd all be better off if he and his siblings sold the ranch to someone who knew what they were doing.

No decisions until after Christmas, he reminded himself.

She directed him to the diner and he parked close to the windows, making sure to lock the truck after they got out. Inside they were bombarded by a cacophony of voices, tinned holiday music, clattering silverware and the unique chinking sound of porcelain plates being stacked together. The waitresses wore jeans with a uniform T-shirt, and bustled by at warp speed. Through it all came the smell of fries and meat and gravy and coffee.

"There's a booth over there. Let's grab it before it's taken," Carrie pointed.

He only picked up bits and pieces of what she said and bit back his frustration. She was pointing toward the back corner, so he assumed she was pointing out a table, and he nodded his agreement. They threaded their way down the aisle to the table. There were times he nearly forgot about his hearing troubles. And then there were days like today that it could be a real challenge. Once, in the store, Carrie had called to him from a different aisle. He hadn't been able to tell which direction the sound had come from.

It would be easier if he could just get a hearing aid or something. But there was nothing that could be done, and that was the most frustrating thing of all.

Their table hadn't been cleared, but the moment they sat down a woman with a blond ponytail bustled over with a plastic dishpan and a cloth and made short work of the mess. "I'll be right back with menus, okay?"

"And this isn't busy?" Duke asked, raising an eyebrow.

"You go to one of those chain restaurants in town and

you'll wait a half hour for a table on a day like today. Trust me. The service here is fast."

Clearly, because menus were in their hands in the next moment, and it wasn't five minutes later and the waitress was back for their orders.

"Not much wonder we were hungry," Duke said, looking down at his watch. "It's after one o'clock."

"Considering how much you got done, that's good time."

"I had a good planner. Not only did you make the list, but you had a strategic plan for navigating the store. You'd have been a good soldier."

"High praise." She leaned back against the cushion of the booth. "So when are you planning to do all this decorating?"

"Tomorrow?" He frowned. "I wanted to do it today, but by the time we get back, it'll be midafternoon. Not a lot of daylight left."

"I could help you tomorrow. Maybe this afternoon you can wrap your gifts."

He smacked his head. "Wrapping paper! That's what I forgot." *What an idiot.*

"I'll cover you. I bought some during the after-Christmas sales last year. I don't have many to wrap, so there's more than enough paper for you, too."

Their food came, so Duke didn't have to reply. But her last words made him think. He'd enjoyed picking out presents today, for his family and his new friends. Carrie had no family…at least none that he knew of.

"So," he said, trying to be super casual, "what about the rest of your family? Do you have any aunts and uncles in the picture? Grandparents?"

She shrugged. "My uncle on my mom's side lives in California with his family. We didn't see him much over the years. Now it's more like a Christmas card in the mail. I have an aunt on my dad's side, but she's in Washington, working for a congressman or something. Dad's parents are gone and my mom's…" She picked up her milkshake glass and took a long sip. "Mom's parents keep in touch, but they moved to Phoenix and a nicer climate. They're getting older and don't like to travel often."

"Would you like to see them?"

Her gaze met his. Sometimes she could be hard to read, as if she pulled down the shades when the topic got too personal. "I miss them," she said simply. "They were around a lot when I was little. They came back to help out a few times when Mom was sick, but it was hard for them. I went out once right after she died, just to get away for a few days. But honestly?" She sighed. "I don't really have the money to take the time off work and pay for the trip."

In that moment Duke knew what he was going to get Carrie for Christmas.

"How's your burger?" he asked, his mind whirring.

"Delicious. Thank you for lunch, Duke."

"Thanks for coming with me today. It was fun." He grinned at her. "So listen. Why don't we stop by your place, grab some of your Christmas stuff and take it all back to my place? We can put in a frozen pizza for a late dinner, have a few beers, watch a movie."

She put down her burger and wiped her fingers on her napkin. "That sounds really nice."

But he detected hesitance in her voice. "Is something wrong?" He put down his fork and leaned forward a bit. "Is this… Our arrangement… Hell," he stammered. "That sounds so bad. What I mean to say is, have things changed for you?"

She glanced up. "No, Duke, they haven't. They haven't changed at all."

So why did she sound so guarded? And why was he getting a weird feeling in the pit of his stomach?

"Good," he answered, picking up his fork again and scooping up some coleslaw. "Because I heard a rumor that *Christmas Vacation* is on TV tonight." A little dose of comedy and pizza might be just what they both needed.

The topic switched to Crooked Valley and ranch business, but Duke couldn't escape the strange feeling he'd gotten when he'd asked her to stay over.

As CARRIE STARED up at the wraparound porch of the big house, the tune to "It's Beginning to Look a Lot Like Christmas" ran through her head. Duke had used a ladder to put the multicolored lights on the eaves, and she'd hung the huge evergreen wreath on the door. The snowman had melted a bit and tipped slightly sideways, looking as if he'd had one too many at the local bar, but still managed to hang on to being upright. Better than that, they'd taken one of the quads to the spruce grove and cut a huge pile of boughs. Then they'd used black twist ties to secure them to the railings on the porch and steps, and Carrie had adorned them with the red bows they'd bought yesterday.

The past twenty-four hours had felt very strange, and yet very right. At times it had almost seemed as though they were a real couple, decorating their place for Christmas. It had felt so…normal.

Except for the constant reminder that their relationship was transient. That she shouldn't get used to spending time with him when he could be gone again before she knew it. All her promises to herself to live in the moment were proving easier said than done. Especially since she'd recognized the depth of her feelings. Saying goodbye to Duke was going to be torture.

Not torture enough to make her end things now, though. It was too good to cut short. As the afternoon waned and the light dimmed slightly, Duke went inside and flicked the switch to the outdoor plug, making the lights come alive.

It was beautiful.

Duke came back outside and jogged down the steps, coming to stand beside her. "So what do you think?" he asked. "We did good, huh?"

She reached for his hand. "It's lovely. I wasn't sure about the multicolored lights instead of white, but you were right. It's so festive!" There was something so happy about the red, green, blue and yellow lights. White said class. But the rainbow of colors was more fun. With the wreath on the door and the evergreen on the railings, the house looked ready for the holidays.

Her breath made clouds in the air, and Duke tugged on her hand, pulling her closer. "I had fun this weekend," he said quietly, looping his arms loosely around her waist. "I wasn't sure I still knew how."

She smiled up at him. "Me, either, really. Do you suppose we both got so caught up in life and responsibilities that we forgot how?"

"Maybe."

He kissed her, slow and soft, making her melt against him. The man knew how to kiss, she'd give him that. And it wasn't exactly a hardship, leaning against his tall, strong form.

"Whew," she said, when the kiss broke off. "I'm not sure the fun's quite over, you keep kissing me like that."

His eyes warmed. "It doesn't have to be."

"Oh?" She'd already spent the night last night. Could be things were getting a little too heavy. She *should* take her stuff and head back to her own house tonight. That was what her brain said anyway. The rest of her wasn't quite on the same wavelength.

"There's always the inside. There's a box of decorations from the attic we can go through."

"Oh, so it's a worker bee you want." She affected a serious face. "I suppose I should be charging you overtime for all this extra work."

But her attempt at a joke fell flat. Duke's face fell, looking slightly stricken at her words. "Carrie, my gosh. Did you do all this because…because I'm your boss and you felt you had to?"

"Of course not! I was just joking, Duke. Really." She reached up with a mittened hand and touched his face. "I know it's strange. You and me, you being the boss, too…but truly, I stayed because I wanted to. It *was* fun. Promise."

He only looked partially appeased. "And the overtime? Are you having trouble making ends meet? Because I can look at the books, see what I can do there…."

"Duke." She said his name firmly, embarrassed that he seemed to know she was struggling financially, more embarrassed that he'd offered to maybe give her a raise. He couldn't do that. She'd feel as if she hadn't earned it, that she just got it because she was sleeping with the boss…

This was the problem with getting involved with him. Too many gray areas.

She looked right into his eyes so he would be in no doubt of her sincerity. "I love that you offered, but truthfully, I'm a big girl. I can take care of myself. You don't need to take care of me. I don't need to be rescued or protected."

He frowned. "Helping isn't rescuing."

"It can be a fine line," she countered. "And you are helping me, in other ways." Heck, if he really wanted to help, he could decide to stay. Take over the ranch. Give them all some stability and peace of mind. Not that she'd say that out loud. She'd promised not to pressure.

He still looked perplexed.

She let out a breath. "Look," she said, quieter now. "I would rather you let me do things on my own. And then, if I need help, I won't feel so bad asking. Does that make any sense?"

"Maybe I just recognize that you've had to do things on your own for a long time. You're so independent. Stubborn."

She knew he meant it in the best possible way, and there was a little stinging behind her eyes. "And that's very sweet of you. Can we just leave it with the idea that if I need something, I'll come to you?"

She wouldn't. Still, it was nice to know she could. If she had to.

"Of course you can." He pulled her close into a hug. "No matter what happens, I'll be there for you."

She wouldn't cry. She wouldn't. She wasn't the crying type. Why on earth did she feel so emotional lately? It had to be the season, and the fact that Duke had opened up a lot of her emotions that she'd held inside. Still, she didn't need to get all crybaby over it. She sniffed and lifted her chin.

"Okay," she said, smiling up at him. "So let's dig out the other stuff and see what we can do."

Chapter Twelve

Duke was still trying to get in touch with Rylan. He'd left several messages on his brother's voice mail, but his call hadn't been returned. Duke waited until after nine at night on the Tuesday following the shopping expedition, hoping to catch Rylan during some downtime. The guy couldn't avoid him forever.

Or maybe he could. His little brother had always been stubborn. Determined to march to his own drummer. Hence the rodeo career.

The phone rang several times and Duke nearly hung up again when there was a click and an annoyed voice in his ear. "Oh, my God. What do you want, Duke?"

"Nice to talk to you, too, bro."

A heavy put-upon sigh. "Whatever."

"Hey. I haven't seen you in nearly two years. What's wrong with touching base?"

"Nothing" came Rylan's agitated reply. "Except it's not just touching base. You want something. Considering the letter that made its way to me a few weeks ago, I figured not answering was my best strategy."

So Rylan wasn't excited about the ranch, either. Of all of them, Duke had thought his brother would be most likely to take to the idea, considering his line of work.

But since Ry was already up in arms about it, Duke

figured the less said about Crooked Valley, the better. "Don't get your panties in a knot," he said. "I was just calling about Christmas."

Rylan groaned. "I'm going to Jamaica."

Duke laughed. "You are not. You're coming here, to the ranch. The whole family is coming."

There was a pause. "You're kidding."

"Lacey's already agreed and is coming out on the twenty-third." He bluffed a little for effect. "And Mom and David are arriving Christmas Eve."

"You got Mom to agree to go out there? She always hated the ranch."

Duke didn't want to out-and-out lie, so he hedged, "It's the first time we'll be together as a family over the holidays in how many years?"

There was silence on the other end for a few moments. "Are you actually thinking of staying there, Duke? Taking over your third? I figured we'd all just let it lapse and sell the place. None of us are ranchers. It's a stupid idea."

Duke leaned his elbows on the kitchen table. "A month or so ago, I would have agreed with you. It's grown on me. A pretty steep learning curve, but I'm enjoying it." It was true. And he owed a lot of that to Carrie. Her enthusiasm and love for the place had rubbed off. "I haven't made any firm decisions, though. I wanted to give it until after the holidays."

Rylan sighed again. "Duke, if you want to stay, I don't know how you're going to keep it. The will said all three of us had to take our place or it would be sold."

And it was clear—neither Lacey nor Rylan was interested. "I haven't figured that out yet." He frowned. The conundrum wasn't something new. He'd been thinking of that for a while. The last thing that would work would be asking Lacey and Rylan to take on their part of the ranch. All three of them were hardheaded. If they were interested in Crooked Valley, they were going to have to come to that conclusion on their own.

Or at least think it.

"Look, it's the first year I've been home from deployment in a long time. Surely we can get together for twenty-four hours. Share the holiday. Eat lots. I'm not asking for a lifetime commitment."

Silence.

"Unless you have other plans?"

"Not anymore," Rylan admitted, a grudging note in his voice. Interesting.

"Great. Can't wait to see you, bro."

"I didn't say yes yet."

Duke grinned. "Yeah, you kinda did."

He clicked off the phone and immediately dialed his mother.

"Hi, Mom."

"Duke! We were just talking about you."

"Talking about Christmas I hope. It's all set."

"Well....actually, we were wondering about the drive. We don't want to get caught on bad roads."

Duke closed his eyes and pressed his fingers to the bridge of his nose. This was why he'd wanted to talk to Rylan first. "Well, we can just watch the forecast. If it's calling for snow, you could always come up a little early. There's plenty of room."

"I don't know, dear..."

"Lacey's coming. So's Ry."

"Your brother's coming?" Her voice perked up, just as he'd known it would. Duke might have been gone overseas a lot, but Rylan was the most distant of the kids. Duke had never really understood why.

"We just got off the phone. Lacey's coming on the twenty-third. I've got lights on the house and a wreath and I'm putting the tree up soon. I've invited a few guests for Christmas morning, too. Quinn, the ranch manager? He has the cutest little girl. Her mom died a while back and so I've invited them to join us. You'll love her. She's cute as a button."

He knew the addition of a child would be a selling point, particularly as none of them had given her grandkids yet.

"You're sure there's lots of room?"

"Positive. I'm staying in the bunkhouse, so the big house is here with all the bedrooms you could want."

"We'll keep an eye on the weather, then," she agreed.

"Perfect." He sat back in his chair. *Thank you, Rylan and Amber,* he thought, smiling. "I'll be in touch," he added, before saying goodbye and hanging up.

The next morning, after the chores were done and everyone set about the day's duties, Duke pulled Carrie aside. "You up for a ride on the quad? I need to chop a Christmas tree. You can help me pick it out."

"Where are you thinking of going? I wanted to check that fence line along the north ridge. I think we're in for colder weather starting tomorrow. But I was going to ride it, not take the ATV."

"I figured it would be easier to tow back if we took the quad."

"You're probably right." She smiled up at him. "You're really going all out for the holidays, aren't you?"

She had no idea. The call to his mother hadn't been his last call of the evening, either. "Everyone's confirmed," he replied. "I even got Rylan to agree to come. It really is going to be a big family Christmas." Bigger than anyone even knew.

"Give me an hour? There are a few things I want to finish up here," she said, and he nodded. He admired her dedication to the ranch and how she always put work first.

"Sure thing. I'll get the stuff together."

He walked out of the barn, whistling tunelessly. Yes, it was all coming together, just the way he planned.

CARRIE TOOK AN inventory of the parts she needed to order for equipment repair. As she scribbled down the supplier and numbers, she couldn't escape the picture of Duke's self-satisfied grin. He was up to something. It was driving her crazy, not knowing what.

Randy walked by, his shoulders hunched against the cold. "Hey," he said stopping in front of her. "Does this mean I'll be getting my hands good and greasy soon?"

Randy was the best man on the place for mechanical work. He seemed to have a natural aptitude for it and he kept the machinery in tip-top shape. "Yep. I'm just making a list of stuff that needs ordering. You got anything you want to add?" She handed over the clipboard.

He wrote down a few things before handing it back. "That should do it. If I think of anything else, I'll let you know."

"Sounds good."

"So," Randy said, shifting his feet a little. "You and Duke, huh?"

She froze. Over the past few weeks she'd told herself that the hands had to know she and Duke were seeing each other. They hadn't been flaunting it, but they hadn't been running around in secret, either. They'd just been…discreet. And yet she'd been caught by surprise, unprepared to answer questions.

"Sorry. I didn't know it was a touchy spot." Randy put up his hands.

"No, it's okay. It's nothing serious, Randy. And completely separate from business. Promise."

"Hey, it's no biggie. We were just wondering, is all. The way you look at each other. We figured there must be something going on."

We. As in…everyone. She was embarrassed but also a little ashamed of how it looked. Boinking the boss. Fabulous. The fact that they'd been having sex for three weeks now…

Her heart stopped. Three weeks. That would mean…

Oh, God.

"Hey, are you okay?" Randy's hand touched her arm. "You went white all of a sudden."

"Sorry." She struggled, attempting to smile and feeling as if somehow she was grimacing. "I don't feel really well at the moment. It just kind of came over me."

"There's a flu going around. You running a fever?" To her chagrin, Randy pulled off a glove and stuck his palm to her forehead. "It doesn't feel like it."

"I'm okay. I probably just didn't eat enough this morning," she answered. "I'm going to go grab something from the fridge."

"Okay, but you let me know if you're not feeling right. We can handle things here if you need to take off and go to bed."

He was being so sweet, despite having pried into personal business. "Thanks," she said, feeling weepy again. But now she knew her unusual emotional reactions lately could have a very real source. A hormonal source. Because according to her calendar, she was approximately ten days late, and she hadn't even considered her cycle. That was how distracted she'd been by Duke.

Oh, God.

"Come to think of it, I'm not feeling great. I'll let Duke know I'm knocking off for the day."

"You got it. Take care, Carrie." They both knew how rare it was for Carrie to take a sick day.

With her stomach churning, Carrie made the walk to the bunkhouse, wondering what on earth she was going to say to Duke. She needn't have worried. He opened the door, saying, "Are you ready to go?"

He then took one look at her face, and followed it up with "What's wrong?"

She would hold it together. She would. She'd tell him she was sick, and then she'd go home and call Kailey and find out for sure before she launched into a full-on panic.

"I'm actually not feeling well. Randy said they can handle the day's work. I'm going to go home, if that's okay."

His eyes darkened with worry. "Why don't you stay here? You can rest here and I'll make you some soup, tea, whatever you want."

She should have foreseen Duke would be kind like that. It made things more complicated. "I appreciate the offer, but...I think I'd like my own bed." It was the first time she'd out-and-out lied to him, but how on earth could she say "I'm going for a pregnancy test" to him?

His frown deepened. "Are you sure?"

"You don't have to look after me, Duke. I'm a big girl, remember?"

"Right." He took a slight step backward. "Well, I hope you feel better."

"Sorry about going to get the tree."

"It'll keep for a day or two."

"You can go without me."

His gaze caught hers and held. "I'd rather wait, if you still want to go."

He wanted to be with her, spend time with her, and she did, too, only this latest wrinkle could truly put this to the test. It complicated everything. Complicated, hell. It blew it right out of the water.

"Let's just see how I am in the morning, okay?" It might turn out to be a nonissue anyway. They'd been careful. Chances were she was just having one of those weird months....

"Okay."

She turned and walked away, not looking back. It was too hard to see his face and still try to wrap her head around the possibility that she could be carrying his child. Having a baby was definitely not in her plans. Not with everything else she had on her plate.

ONCE SHE WAS home she called Kailey, asking her to come over. Kailey was busy like everyone else, but as soon as Carrie hiccuped over the word *emergency,* the phone clicked and ten minutes later Kailey was at her door, hair in a ratty braid, smelling like the horse barn.

"What the hell's going on?" she called, walking through the door without knocking. "Are you all right?"

"I'm in here." Carrie sat in the living room, cradling a cup of tea. "You want tea? Water's still hot."

"Tea? You look more like you need a shot of bourbon. You got any? What happened? Did things go bad with you and Duke? Do I need to go mess him up?"

Carrie wondered if she looked as miserable as she felt when she looked up into Kailey's face. "Duke's been wonderful," she said quietly. "And I'm late."

Those three words took the wind out of Kailey's

sails, and she dropped to sit on a footstool. "Pregnant? Oh, jeez, Carrie."

"I know." She started welling up again and stomped a foot, sloshing a little tea. "I've felt fine! I haven't been sick. But I feel like crying at the worst times! I was watching TV the other night and one of those long-distance commercials came on and I was a blubbering mess. How stupid is that?"

Kailey smiled indulgently. "Getting emotional doesn't mean you're knocked up. Honey, have you ever thought that maybe being in love is doing it to you? I love you, but you hold your feelings so close. Now they're all coming out, you see?"

She was initially startled that Kailey seemed to read her feelings so well. But perhaps there was some truth to the theory. "That's not much better, though, is it? This isn't supposed to be about love!"

"So." Kailey reached over and took one of Carrie's hands. "The first thing we'd better do is get you a test. Maybe you have nothing to worry about."

Carrie sipped at her hot tea. "Are you up for a drive? I don't want to get the test here in town. It's like taking out an advertisement. I do *not* need people speculating about me. About Duke. About us."

"I'll do you one better than that. We'll go to the women's clinic in the city. Everything's totally confidential and they'll do the test while you wait."

Carrie looked into Kailey's eyes. "You seem to be very sure of that."

"I've had a scare before."

"Right." Carrie swallowed, briefly wondering why this was the first time she was hearing about Kailey's scare but too concerned with her immediate problem to get into it. "You're sure it's confidential?"

"Positive. Come on, get your coat. I'll drive."

Carrie went through the motions for the next hour and a half. First the drive, then the wait at the clinic, then peeing in the cup and waiting for the results. When they came, Kailey was sitting beside her.

"Well, Ms. Coulter, it seems your test is positive."

She looked up in the nurse's face, the words echoing in her ears. "You're sure?"

The nurse's kind eyes softened. "It's very rare to have a false positive. I take it this wasn't expected."

Carrie shook her head, her throat too tight to speak.

"Well, nothing has to be decided right away. When you're ready, we have referral services for whatever option you might choose for the pregnancy. I know it's a lot to take in right now, so let's just go over the basics."

The nurse gently went over diet, symptoms Carrie might experience in the days to come, the importance of a follow-up appointment and a handful of literature for her to read regarding her options. Kailey helped her make an appointment for the following month and tucked the card with the details in Carrie's purse. "Come on," Kailey said softly. "Let's get you home."

All through the drive, Carrie's mind was racing. She was going to have a baby. The timing was so wrong. Everything was so wrong. How could she afford to have a child? How could she do the job she did with a little baby? Yes, Quinn did it, but Amber was older. Old enough for day care. How could she afford the medical bills associated with having a baby, on top of the ones she was still paying off for her mom? After the baby came, how could she possibly pay all those bills and pay for day care, too?

Then there was Duke. He made a good show of things and she'd allowed herself to hope, but the truth was she wasn't sure he meant to stay. He had such a code of honor that she knew he'd insist on supporting his child. Which might help with the initial cash problem, but also created new ones. What if Duke stayed at Crooked Valley, made it his home? How would she know if he'd done it because he wanted to, and not because he'd felt obligated because of their child? She loved him, but she wanted him to love her, too. Not out of duty, but because he just did.

She'd been forced into things by circumstances her whole life. She didn't want to put that on Duke, too. He'd been manipulated enough by Joe, just to get him to set foot on the ranch in the first place. He couldn't know about the baby. Not until he figured out what he wanted.

Kailey stayed quiet until they got back home. "Come on," she said gently, pocketing the keys. "You're not staying alone tonight."

"I'm not?"

"No, you're not. You're going to go inside and run a warm bath while I make us something to eat. You're going to put on your fuzziest pajamas and come out and we're going to chill. We can watch a movie or talk or whatever you want to do. But I'm staying."

Carrie took a deep breath, utterly grateful for Kailey's loyalty, her kindness. "You're a good friend, K. The best."

"I know that. And I know if this were me, you'd do the same. So come on. Let me take care of you for today."

She did. Numbly, she followed Kailey into the house. She took off her shoes and got fleece pajamas out of her drawer as Kailey started the bathwater running. Steam began filling the bathroom and Carrie shivered as she undressed and got into the hot tub. The water eased into her muscles as she sank lower and let herself relax.

And it was then, only then, that the feelings rose to the surface and she started to cry.

Chapter Thirteen

Carrie couldn't afford to take more than a day off work, so the next morning she shooed Kailey out of the house, insisting she'd be fine. The cry in the tub had done wonders, and so had talking to Kailey. She'd let out all her insecurities and fears, and while Kailey didn't have the answers, she'd been a kind and supportive ear.

Carrie knew she had to tell Duke, but not yet. What would be the harm in waiting a few weeks after all? She could use the time to sort through her own feelings. And Duke could use it to decide what he wanted to do about Crooked Valley.

By midmorning she was exhausted and paused for a break when Duke came out of the big house and made his way to the barn. "You're feeling better?" he called out, and the sound of his voice sent a shiver of pleasure along her nerve endings.

She had no defenses against this man. And she was carrying his child.

"Much, thanks," she called back, hunching her shoulders against the wind. Duke was several feet away but close enough she could lower her voice to a normal level. "A day of rest did wonders."

He got a strange look on his face but it soon passed.

"That's good," he replied, but his eyes still looked wary. Good heavens, was her guilt written all over her face?

Maybe she should just tell him.

And then she remembered the soft way he'd smiled at Amber, how protective he tended to get whether he realized it or not. If he knew she was pregnant, would he get all weird about the physical labor required in her job? She'd like to think no, but the truth was she just wasn't sure. And right now the stability of this job was all she could count on.

"Did you get your tree?" she asked.

"I did. Do you want to see it? It's a beauty. Eight feet tall. With the star on the top, I bet it'll just about touch the ceiling in the family room."

"It sounds lovely."

"It'll be more lovely when it's decorated." The awkward moment seemed to have passed, and he reached for her hand. "Maybe after work you'd like to come in. I put a chicken and vegetables in the Crock-Pot this morning. We could have some dinner at the main house and decorate it. Do it up right."

Funny how, before yesterday, her answer would have been an automatic yes. Now she was hesitant to spend too much time with him. To get too comfortable. At the same time she craved his company.

She bit down on her lip. It wasn't just about staying on the ranch. It was really starting to sink in that having this baby meant that she'd be connected to Duke for the rest of her life—whether or not they ended up together. If they did, she'd always wonder if it was because of the baby. And if they didn't, she'd have to see him all the time, knowing how she felt about him and unable to have him.

What a freaking mess.

"Carrie, what is it? I can tell something's bothering you." He came forward and curled a gloved hand around her neck, pulling her close. "It's more than a flu bug. More than whatever had you feeling poorly yesterday. Let me help."

Let me help. She was starting to know him better. He'd come to Crooked Valley and put himself at the mercy of herself and Quinn because they knew ranching. But they were still in no doubt of who was the boss. What Duke knew was how to be in charge. He wouldn't just help. He'd take over. She wasn't quite ready for that yet.

"I'm fine, I promise. Just a lot on my mind." She looked up at him. "This time of year is difficult." It wasn't exactly a lie. More of a particular wording to lead him to a specific conclusion.

"I should have thought of that." His eyes were soft with compassion. "Still, come on in for dinner. Make a new memory." His face loomed closer, the urge to kiss him greater. Her breath gathered in her chest and held, painful anticipation of the contact to come. When his lips touched hers it was as if all the best parts of Christmas mingled with all the bittersweet bits. And he had no idea of the turmoil inside her as she kissed him back, sliding one gloved hand over his shoulder as she tipped her face to his.

A discreet cough echoed through the still, frosty air and Carrie pulled back, heat rushing to her cheeks. Hadn't it just been days ago that she'd been worried about what the guys would say if they knew she was messing around with the boss? Hadn't she been worried about undermining her authority as foreman? Boy, she'd been stupid. She'd gotten involved. She'd fallen head over heels.

"Dinner sounds good," she murmured. "But I have to go."

"Sure," Duke replied. "Sure thing."

And she walked away without looking at him again.

DUKE HAD PUT some effort into dinner, Carrie could see that the moment she walked in the door. Candlelight flickered from the kitchen and the casual table and chairs there, but there was nothing casual about the table setting. He'd set it carefully with Joe and Eileen's white dishes, red plaid napkins, candles and good glassware. As she paused to take in the romantic scene, Duke took a bottle of white wine from the fridge and put it on the table, perfectly chilled.

"Dinner's almost ready," he said, and her mouth watered from the delicious scent of roast chicken and vegetables.

"You didn't have to cook for me," she said, folding her hands in front of her.

"I like to cook, as long as I can keep it simple," he stated, and he took a platter and added carved chicken, potatoes and golden carrots. "The Crock-Pot is great. I put it on earlier and could work around all day without worrying about it. Whoever invented it is a genius."

She excused herself to freshen up, and when she came back to the kitchen, Duke had uncorked the wine and poured it into two glasses. She took her seat at the table and tried very hard to act natural.

For a few moments they filled their plates, and when they finally paused, Duke raised his glass. "To a Crooked Valley Christmas," he toasted, smiling at her.

She smiled back and picked up her glass, grossly uncomfortable now but determined to fake things as long as she could. "To Christmas," she echoed softly.

But Duke didn't drink. "And to us," he added, catching her gaze in the candlelight.

Her throat tightened. "To us," she whispered, and while Duke drank from his glass, she touched hers to her lips only. The taste of the tart wine swept across her tongue as she licked her lips, but she didn't swallow any. Instead she put down her glass and picked up her knife and fork. "This looks delicious."

Dinner went fine. The chicken was succulent and flavorful; the vegetables rich with the herbs from the chicken and broth. A fire crackled in the fireplace and Carrie knew she couldn't ask for anything more. It was that perfection that had her on edge, though, always wary. One day and the secret knowledge was driving her crazy. She wasn't good with secrets. She was a "what you see is what you get" kind of woman, and it didn't sit well that she was deliberately hiding the truth from Duke—even though she knew, intellectually, that twenty-four hours could hardly constitute keeping something from him. Wasn't it right that she should figure some things out first?

"You're not drinking the wine," Duke observed as their plates emptied. "Don't you like it?"

"Oh," she answered, startled. "It's fine. I'm just... just not much in the mood for it tonight." She swallowed against the lie building in her mouth. "The food was great, but maybe it's too soon for the wine to agree with me."

"Oh, I should have considered that," Duke apologized, smiling at her. "Glad the food met with your approval, though."

She looked down at her plate. It was cleaned down to the last teaspoon of gravy. One thing was for sure—

pregnancy had only sharpened her appetite, not dimin-
ished it.

"So what about this tree, then?" Changing the subject was the best bet, so she stood, smiled and began
collecting their dirty dishes.

"Right, the tree." A smile lit his face. "Well, actually, I put the lights on before you showed up. So now
it's just the garland and ornaments that need to go on."

"You're the soul of efficiency, Duke. I never would
have pegged you for the sentimental holiday type."

He grabbed the platter and started putting away leftovers as she put their dishes in the dishwasher. "Me,
either, really. I think it's being home, and knowing everyone is coming that's doing it. It'll be the first time
we've all been together in…well, I don't know how
many years." He paused behind her and put his hands
on her shoulders. "And I think maybe it's you, too. This
is the first year in a long time I've had someone to celebrate Christmas with. You've brought out my latent
sentimental side." He chuckled against her hair, sending delightful shivers down her back.

She moved out of his embrace, closed the dishwasher
and went to examine the boxes of decorations. Gold
garland was shoved into a bag in the corner of the box,
and she pulled it out. "I think if we loop this around,
it'll work fine." She pulled out three, four, five balls of
garland and grinned. "I think Joe was fond of big trees."

Duke laughed and came to her aid. "Here. I'll start on
the top branches. Let's plug in the lights first, though,
so we can see what we're doing."

He plugged the lights into the receptacle and the
room was filled with pinpoints of colorful light. Duke
hadn't scrimped. There were hundreds of them, reds,

blues, greens, yellows, all sparkling from the branches of the spruce tree. "Oh, Duke. Those are beautiful."

"Wait'll we get the rest on," he said, standing back.

She grabbed another strand of garland and they worked their way around the branches, swooping and hanging scallops of sparkly garland on the evergreen branches. When they got to the bottom, Duke retrieved the box of ornaments and put them on the floor between them.

"Okay, go to town," he advised, angling her a sideways grin.

They hung the glass balls with care. Interspersed with the more "formal" decorations were ones that Carrie could only assume had sentimental value. A miniature dream catcher. A maroon-and-white ball with the logo of the Colorado Avalanche, Joe's favorite hockey team. Handmade horseshoe ornaments hung with red satin ribbon. Then Duke's hand slowed as he reached into the box and pulled out a black-and-gold ornament. He held it up to the light and Carrie saw a suspicious glint in his eyes.

"Duke? What is it?"

He carefully placed the ornament in his hand. On one side was a star that said U.S. Army. On the other it said There's Strong. Then There's Army Strong.

She didn't know what to say. Perhaps Duke thought that Joe hadn't cared. Maybe now he'd understand that his grandfather had cared more than he'd ever let on. That he was proud of his son—and his grandson.

"He really did care, didn't he?"

Her eyes stung. Damn these hormones! It had to be that making her emotional. It couldn't be Duke. It couldn't be the feelings she had for him....

Except she knew that it could.

"He cared," she said simply. "I think maybe, looking back, he didn't know how to show it after all the time had passed."

"I always felt like he'd expected something we couldn't give."

"Maybe, Duke, he wanted it for himself. But he understood you had to be yourself. Maybe that's why he left the ranch the way he did. To give you guys a chance at it—if you wanted it."

Duke carefully hung the ornament on the tree, then stood back. He held out his hand to her and she took it, afraid of this thing growing between them. It was no longer about enjoying the moment. He had no idea how deep her feelings ran.

"I'm still figuring that out," he said quietly. "It's a big decision. But I'm glad I came back. If I hadn't, I wouldn't have met you again."

All evening she'd been wondering if she should tell him about the baby. Just when she thought she should, he came out with a reminder that he was undecided. The last thing he needed was more pressure to get stuck in a life he didn't want.

"I'm glad I met you, too, Duke. Again." She smiled up at him hesitantly.

His brow furrowed. "Carrie, what is it? You've been acting strangely since yesterday. I know something's bothering you." He pulled on her hand and tugged her over to the sofa to sit down. "You weren't really sick yesterday, were you?"

"What do you mean?" Her pulse rate picked up beneath his intense gaze.

"I went by your place last night to check on you, about nine o'clock. Kailey's car was in your yard and the lights were all on."

"She came to make sure I was all right." It wasn't a lie.

He was silent for a long time. "Carrie, if you want out, please be honest with me. We agreed that if it didn't work for either of us we'd speak up. It won't change your position here on the ranch. I promise."

He was giving her a way out when, if she was being truthful with herself, out was the last thing she wanted. "Do you want to call it quits, Duke?"

"Nothing's changed for me," he assured her without hesitation.

Hope. That was what that little lift beneath her rib cage was. She squeezed his fingers. "For me, either."

"Then what happened yesterday? What's going on today? It feels like you're here, but you're somewhere else, too."

She took a deep breath. "Before I say anything, I want you to know that..." She struggled to find the right words. "This shouldn't have any bearing on the decision you need to make about the ranch, okay? Promise me."

He pulled back and stared at her. "What in the world are you talking about?"

Her heart was hammering now, painful against the wall of her chest. "Promise me," she demanded.

"Fine. I promise."

Carrie met his gaze. She'd never been so afraid of anything in her whole life—and that included the time she'd come face-to-face with a hungry mountain lion.

"I wasn't exactly sick yesterday."

He looked into her eyes, nodded encouragingly. "Okay."

"I called Kailey and we..." Oh, God, why was this so hard? *Because it's important,* a voice inside her reminded her. *It's huge. You're going to be parents together.*

"You?"

She let out her breath. "Kailey took me to a clinic and I had a pregnancy test."

He schooled his features, but not before she got a glimpse of pure, unadulterated terror. She tried to remind herself that she'd had much the same reaction, but it stung just the same. This should be a happy time. A time of shared rejoicing, not a time of shock and then dealing with a…a mistake.

"And it was positive?" he asked faintly.

"I'm afraid so."

He uttered a succinct curse under his breath and sank back against the couch cushions. "But we were careful."

"I know."

"God." He put his hand to his forehead. "Just…oh. Wow."

"I'm sorry, Duke. I hadn't even thought of it until yesterday when I realized I was late. I'm just as shocked as you are."

He closed his eyes.

Hers watered. Again. She blinked and forced the emotion away. Last night she'd cried enough. Today she had to be strong.

"You need time to let it soak in," she suggested, and went to push herself off the sofa. His hand darted out, though, and gripped her by the wrist, staying her exit.

"Don't go. We need to talk about this. About…oh, man, Carrie. I'm going to be a dad."

"I know," she whispered.

His eyes opened and he looked right at her. "You're going to be a mom."

"Yes." The very idea sent panic streaking through

her, but something else, too. Something wonderful and big and protective and fantastic—and that feeling was equally as scary as finding out the news in the first place.

"Don't go. Stay. Just…let me be for a few minutes, let this soak in. Give me a little time."

She waited. It was torturous, but she waited in the soft light of the Christmas tree with the fire crackling in the background. She was pretty sure this wasn't the evening he'd planned for them.

He finally spoke, so softly she had to lean forward to hear. "I've been waiting for a sign. Something to tell me what I should do. Looks like I got my wish."

"No!" She stood up quickly, before he had time to grab her arm again. "You promised. This has nothing to do with Crooked Valley."

"It has everything to do with Crooked Valley! I'm one-third owner and you're the foreman. How can I possibly leave knowing you're here with our baby? What kind of man do you take me for?"

"Whether you stay on the ranch has nothing to do with me! It has to be right for you. Can't you see that?" She put her hands to her face for a brief moment, trying to regain control. Oh, she should have listened to her head and waited. "Please, please don't make this decision based on a baby. What a burden to put on his or her shoulders. On my shoulders."

"On yours?"

If they were going to be honest, they might as well go all the way. "I know you like me, Duke. I know you like spending time with me. That we've got this chemistry going on. But do you love me?"

His face flattened in surprise and he didn't answer right away. Disappointment sat heavily on her, but she was somehow glad she'd asked. Now at least she knew and could proceed knowing she was right.

"I don't want you to stay at Crooked Valley out of obligation. You're our baby's father and you always will be, no matter if you're at the ranch or not."

She believed her words 100 percent. And yet a part of her still felt like weeping, knowing that she was pregnant and the father of her child didn't love her. Not the same way she cared for him.

"I have responsibilities…."

Her heart ached a little more each time he opened his mouth, confirming that Duke was used to a life of fulfilling his duty but only that. Duty.

"Which you can fulfill whether you're at the ranch or not. You promised, Duke. I'm going to hold you to it. I don't want you making decisions out of some weird sense of duty."

He stood up, came to her. "I can't just separate one from the other. It's not that easy, Carrie. I need time. Time to think everything through. Time to decide what's best for everyone."

And though it killed her to say it, she knew she had to utter the next words. "Duke, you're not in the army anymore. The chain of command doesn't apply here. You don't get to decide for me. If you try to, I'll…I'll quit."

Which was just about the dumbest thing she could have said at this moment. Where would she go? What would she do? She had no family to go to. No one…

Phoenix. Her grandparents were still there. As much as it would kill her to leave the ranch, she could probably beg them for a place to stay until she found a job and got on her feet.

Her heart broke a little just thinking of it. She loved

this place. It was as much her home as it was Duke's. Maybe more so.

"Don't get yourself worked up," he said, his voice taut with strain. "We'll figure it out. There's time, right? You can't be more than a few weeks along…"

Not more than a few weeks. Time enough for everything to be knocked on its head.

"Not far along at all." The words echoed hollowly through the room.

Duke let out a big breath and suddenly smiled. "A baby," he repeated, as if the news was brand-new again.

Some of the tension started to release in Carrie's chest. Duke's smile distracted her enough that she was unprepared for his next edict.

"From now on you're not taking any chances, you hear? We've gotta keep that baby safe. No more riding to check the lines, and you're going to take it easy in the barn."

It only took a second for what he was saying to sink in, but as soon as it did, Carrie stood back and put her hands on her hips.

"Like hell," she said through gritted teeth.

Chapter Fourteen

Duke stared at Carrie. She was so angry. So...defensive. He frowned at her as she faced off against him. She'd always been a reasonable person. Surely she could see the logic in what he'd just said.

"Come on," he said, his voice the tiniest bit incredulous. "You know what I'm saying makes sense. You can't just carry on as before. Your job is physically demanding—"

"For a woman? Is that what you were going to say?"

Irritation flared. Could he say nothing right tonight? "I'm just asking you to be careful! Not to take unnecessary chances!" He stepped forward but then halted abruptly. He hadn't asked her the most important question of all. He'd plowed right over top of it but now it fell like a sledgehammer in his brain, refusing to move.

"That is," he said, quieter, his heart seizing a bit, "if you're planning on seeing the pregnancy through."

And then he held his breath.

He'd never given serious thought to the abortion issue before, but he did now. And what he realized was that it was her body, but it was their baby, and whatever decision she made affected him, too. Whatever the outcome, he wanted to be a part of it.

"I'm seeing it through," she answered, her voice barely above a whisper.

Relief sluiced through him, more relief than he'd expected to feel. "Okay," he said, while his knees felt wobbly. "Okay."

"Duke," she said, and he could tell she was working hard on keeping her voice calm. "You can't start telling me what I can or can't do. You can't monitor every activity or what I eat or where I go. It doesn't work that way."

He knew she was right. And yet he was still the tiniest bit angry. Angry that she was so stubborn that she'd stand her ground even if he made valid points. "I'm just asking that you be sensible," he argued. "Take care. Not put yourself in a position where you could get hurt or overdo it."

"I think I know my limits," she retorted.

His head was starting to hurt. He'd wanted a quiet supper, decorating the tree, some time alone with her. He hadn't bargained for this; hadn't prepared for it. He was still coming to terms with all the other changes in his life and now he was going to be a father. He was trying desperately to wrap his head around it.

"I think I should go for now, before we really get in an argument," she suggested sadly. "Thanks for dinner, Duke, but I'm going to head home. Get some sleep. Do some thinking. You need time to do that, too."

He did. Because right now the answer seemed so obvious to him and she was having none of it.

"I don't want to argue with you," he answered, following her to the kitchen, leaving the mess of boxes and unused ornaments behind. "If you're keeping the baby, you must realize that some activities are riskier than others."

She spun around and faced him, her eyes flashing. "Do you suppose I don't know that? Do you think I'm that stupid, or do you think I don't care?"

Her questions stopped him in his tracks. "I know you're not stupid. And I can see that you care."

"Then maybe you can trust me?"

He stared at her. He understood what she was saying, just as he understood his warnings were also justified.

He also now understood the impulse to make things right. If it was anyone but Carrie, he'd probably be offering marriage so that their child could have a two-parent home. Carrie would tell him what he could do with his offer—he was equally sure of that fact. She wouldn't settle for that sort of arrangement—and he knew she was right about that, too. Children deserved parents who loved each other. Who were committed to each other, not just joined by a baby. So what was he supposed to do? It seemed as though there was no right answer he could give.

"Are you feeling okay?" he murmured, wanting to know. His child was inside her right now and it made him feel both larger than life and petrified.

She nodded. "I'm doing all right. But now you understand why I didn't have any wine."

So many changes. How could he just walk away in January? How could he stay and not keep the ranch?

"Let's just take a few days to let things settle," he suggested, his heart sinking. "How does that sound?"

"Sensible," she replied, her face relaxing a little. "No rash decisions. We have to be smart about this."

Duke looked down at her. She spoke with such authority that she gave the appearance of being in perfect control. On closer examination, though, he saw the uncertainty in her eyes. Despite her outward bravado, he got the feeling she was scared to death.

He reached out and pulled her close, enveloping her in a hug. She was surprised and stiffened in his arms at first, but then, with a heavy sigh, she relaxed and let him hold her, spreading her hands across his back.

"I'm sorry," he murmured against her hair. "It's a lot to take in. You're not in this alone, though, okay? Will you remember that? We'll figure it out."

She nodded against his shoulder.

"Do you want to stay? You're welcome to. We can just watch TV or something."

Carrie pushed out of his arms. "Thanks, but I think I just want to go home. I'm tired. It's been a crazy few days."

He nodded. Walked her to the door, saw her out. After her truck left the driveway, though, he stood on the cold veranda, his hands in his jeans pockets, shoulders hunched against the chill.

Fun. It was only supposed to be fun. Dancing, hanging out, laughing, great sex. No commitments, no expectations. No consequences.

Except there were consequences. Big ones. Ones that tied him to Carrie—and to this ranch—for years to come.

That should be freaking him out more than it was. The biggest surprise was that what was really bothering him was how, in the blink of an eye, their relationship had changed. There was a distance now that felt impossible to bridge—brought on by something that should bring two people closer together.

He sighed, his breath forming a frosty cloud. Maybe he and Carrie really had been fooling themselves into thinking they had something special. Because here they were, at the first sign of trouble, further apart than ever.

AS THE HOLIDAYS drew closer, it seemed to Carrie that she and Duke got further apart.

She had taken a crew out just this morning and they'd shifted the herd into another pasture, where fresh stacks of hay were waiting. Now she was tired and chilled right to the bone, warming herself in front of the potbellied stove located in the barn office. Jack's wife had sent in a tin of Christmas cookies, and while Carrie didn't have much of a taste for coffee these days, she'd heated herself a mug of apple cider in the small microwave. They were talking about holiday plans when another pair of boots sounded outside the room.

Carrie turned around to see Duke standing in the doorway. "Hey, guys," he greeted.

"Hey, boss," Randy replied, handing over the tin. "Want a cookie?"

"Don't mind if I do," he answered, stepping inside and reaching for a sweet. "Cold one out there today."

"Yessir," Jack replied, and Carrie was struck by the deference with which they spoke to Duke. It was with respect—as a leader and a boss. Maybe he still had a lot to learn, but he'd earned their trust and confidence.

He was a good man. A good man who hadn't really made much of an effort where she was concerned lately. She'd asked for time. They'd both needed it to come to grips with what they were dealing with. Still, she hadn't quite expected it to be so easy for him. That stung a little bit.

"Carrie, you got a few minutes?"

His voice interrupted her thoughts and she looked up. "Yeah. No problem." She took her mug with her—

the cider was keeping her fingers warm—and stepped out into the corridor with him.

"What can I do for you?"

He led her away from the office, a good distance down the barn and a good deal colder, too. When they were far enough away that they wouldn't be heard, Duke halted and faced her.

"I just wanted to know how you're feeling. If everything's okay."

She swallowed against a little ball of emotion. His concern was genuine, written all over his face. She wished she knew how to stop loving him. It was clear now that he cared for her but didn't love her. It would be easier to get over him and get on with what needed to be done if he'd be disagreeable. Turn into a jerk... instead of being so conscientious and caring.

"I'm right as rain, Duke. I feel a little tired sometimes, and the Christmas commercials on TV make me weepy, but I'm not experiencing any morning sickness or anything. My job keeps me active, and I'm trying to eat well and get lots of sleep."

"Good."

His expression changed, turning apprehensive. "Look," he said, lowering his voice a touch, "I don't know how to diplomatically put this, so I'm just going to ask. Do you need money for anything? The doctor? Vitamins? Anything at all?"

"No," she answered, looking down at her toes. "I'm fine." So matter-of-fact. So far he'd covered doctor and banker, when that wasn't what she wanted from him at all.

"I've been thinking a lot since you told me about the baby." He spoke quietly, and she lifted her head again to look into his face. "You're single and alone and I know you live day-to-day financially. I'm sure you considered your options. I know your road ahead doesn't look easy, Carrie. I admire your bravery."

She chuckled, but it was a humorless sound of disbelief. "Bravery? The decision was taken out of my hands, don't you think?"

He shrugged. "You could have made a different decision. One that might have made things easier down the road."

And she'd considered it—briefly. In the end she knew she'd have regrets. She thought of Quinn and all the pain he'd been through, but how he constantly insisted that he had no regrets about being a single parent even though things were really hard without Marie. She might not have family but she had friends, and she was strong. She'd muddle through.

She'd do better than muddle, damn it. She'd make sure they had a good life. A life filled with love and laughter, even if they had to live simply.

He reached out and took her hand. "Carrie, I've been thinking a lot over the past few days. Thinking about what I want and our situation and I keep coming up with the same thing. It doesn't make sense for me to go somewhere else. Where am I going to go? I've enjoyed my time at Crooked Valley. I've enjoyed my time with you. And of course, my son or daughter will be here."

On some level she'd known this was coming. Duke might have shown up here at loose ends, but that was an anomaly for him. From the beginning, she'd known he was the kind of man used to having a plan and a purpose.

"So you're just going to settle?"

"It's not settling. I came home to find out what I

wanted. What if what I want is right in front of me? Wouldn't it be stupid to let it go?"

"Duke, you're used to having a mission. You're used to being needed, to having a problem to solve or an objective to take. I can't be another one of your missions. That's not what I want."

"That's not what I'm doing."

"Oh? Then answer me this. If I'd never gotten pregnant, would you have decided to stay here?"

"But you are pregnant. It changes everything."

Her heart physically hurt as she looked up at him. "No, it doesn't. You're letting it cloud everything else. You need to separate things to see them clearly. How you feel about ranching. How you feel about me. Those are separate from how you feel about becoming a father."

"I already told you I've enjoyed the ranch…"

"And what about me, Duke?"

He smiled then, all easy charm. "You know how I feel about you."

Oh, she was so mixed-up. Her body warmed beneath his gaze and intimate smile. And yet part of her ran cold, knowing he was avoiding the real question she was asking, knowing he was avoiding it because they both knew the answer. She wanted to believe him. It would be easier than holding out for what she wanted—what she needed. In the end, though, she knew the easy way wouldn't make her happy.

So she stepped back, pulling her hands from his. "You're right. I do know how you feel. I know you care about me. I know we enjoyed being together. I know we had fun. But you don't love me, Duke. And I can't lie to myself and pretend that you do so that it makes everything all right."

The smile slid from his face. "Carrie…"

"I know," she said quietly, knowing his gaze was fully on her face and there was no doubt he was getting her words. "It hasn't been that long. It's too early for love. I know, Duke. But for my own peace of mind and stress level, I think it would be best if we just kept our relationship as boss-employee. For now."

"You don't want to see me anymore."

She didn't know how to say it without revealing too much. Like how every time he touched her it reminded her that the depth of her feelings weren't returned. How could she possibly endure making love to him again knowing he didn't feel the same way she did?

"There's not much point in dragging things out. We made a deal."

"A deal?" His brow puckered.

Why did this have to be so hard? It was taking all her strength to appear in control when inside she felt as if she was shattering. It was supposed to be fun. No strings. Chemistry. She should have known better. She *had* known better, but she'd chosen to lie to herself instead.

"We agreed that, if at any point it wasn't working, we'd could call it off, no hard feelings." She met his gaze. "It's not working for me, Duke."

Only not in the way he thought. It wasn't that she didn't care. It was that she was in way over her head. Heart, body and soul.

"You don't mean that. Maybe if we just gave it more time… It's a lot to get used to." He reached for her again, putting his palm against her cold cheek. "Being with you is…amazing. I'm not ready to call it quits yet."

She closed her eyes, enjoying the caress for a brief moment before saying what she needed to say.

"I'm sorry, Duke. That's not enough for me." She took a step back. "I've got to get back to work."

She was six feet away when his voice followed her. "I'm not giving up, Carrie."

She turned around and faced him so he'd be sure to understand her words. "Don't make this harder than it has to be, Duke," she said, then turned again and forced one foot after the other as she left the barn into the cold December morning.

She didn't cry; she was pretty sure she didn't have any tears left after the past several days. She'd made her point, said what she'd needed to say. They'd had an affair and it had been great, but it was time to get back to real life. And that meant freeing Duke to make the decision he needed to make without her being in the middle, confusing the issue.

The house stood before her, homey and welcoming with the decorations they'd put up for the holidays. Carrie nearly wished that she'd never followed him out of the Silver Dollar that night. She'd realized then that actions had consequences. If only she'd known what her consequences would be, the amount of hurt that she was about to put herself through, the way her life would change…

She *nearly* wished it, but not quite. Because deep down she couldn't find it in her heart to be sorry for finding love after all this time—even if it wasn't returned.

Chapter Fifteen

The weather forecast for December 23 was looking grim, with blowing snow due to hit midafternoon and linger into Christmas Eve. Quinn let the hands go at noon, but he and Carrie stayed to finish out the day—at least until the snow started. Then they'd go home—Quinn to pick up Amber, Carrie to her little house, and they'd hunker down until the storm passed. Duke was at the ranch to look after the stock in the barn.

Shortly after their lunch break, a car rolled into the yard. Lacey, arriving right on time for the holidays. Quinn stared across the barnyard as Lacey waved in their direction. Carrie waved back, then watched as Lacey took a bag from her car as well as a sack of presents and made her way up to the house.

It looked as if Duke was going to have his family Christmas after all. Carrie still wasn't sure what she was doing for the big day. She knew her invitation from Duke was still open. But he'd done exactly as she'd asked. He'd given her distance.

"You okay?" Quinn asked quietly, right by her shoulder.

"Yeah, sure. Why wouldn't I be?" She pasted on a smile for his benefit and reached up, pulling her hat down over her ears.

"Oh, I don't know. The past while you and Duke have hardly said two words to each other. Trouble in paradise?"

She met Quinn's eyes. "Something like that."

"You want to talk about it?"

She chuckled. "You're a guy. You don't want to hear about girl drama."

"Carrie, you've got less drama than any woman I've ever known. If it's bothering you, it must be important."

She teetered on the edge of confiding in him, but held off. So far the only person besides Duke who knew about the baby was Kailey. She wasn't sure Quinn wouldn't try to curtail her activities, as well. "I'm okay for now, but thanks for the offer," she replied. She nudged him with her elbow. "Besides, I saw you staring at Lacey."

"Hmph." He grumbled and turned his back on the house. "I know Duke wasn't keen on coming home, but Lacey doesn't even pretend to like the ranch. Whatever."

Carrie laughed. It was good to bug Quinn and take her mind off herself for a bit.

"Listen, I'm going to take Sage and go give the herd one last check. You go, pick up Amber, have a lazy afternoon."

"Are you sure? I could go with you. Snow's not far off, Carrie. You don't want to get caught in it."

But Carrie had been doing this long enough that she could read the weather. "It's a good hour, hour and a half out. And I'm just going to be at the near pasture. First sign of flakes, I'll boot it for home. Promise."

Quinn shrugged. "Best get going, then."

At least one person at Crooked Valley had confidence in her abilities, she thought. Quinn didn't worry about her overdoing or showing bad judgment.

Quinn also didn't know she was pregnant.

She had Sage saddled in a jiffy, and she pulled up her collar against the stiff wind as they started out. This was going to be a quick check indeed. With any luck, the cattle would already be taking shelter from the wind in the treed areas that climbed the foothills. Then she could go home, unwind with some cocoa, a hot bath and a holiday DVD.

LACEY HAD BROUGHT not only presents for everyone but bags of groceries, too. "I'm a decent cook, you know," she asserted, and began unpacking supplies. Tomatoes, ground beef, ricotta cheese, fresh pasta and herbs. "I'm going to make a lasagna for dinner that will make you weep with gratitude."

"Right," Duke said, raising an eyebrow. Then he laughed and scooped her up into a hug. "I'm glad you're here, Lace."

She smacked his shoulder. "Hey, put me down! What did you do with my grouchy brother? Jeez."

He put her down, but the mood was light as she started making a mess around the stove.

Quinn stomped in, and Duke heard voices behind him. He went down the hall to check things out and stopped short at the sight of his mother, Helen, and her husband, David, standing in the foyer. "Mom!"

His mother had grayed a bit since he'd last seen her, and had a few more wrinkles around her eyes, but she was the same mom. Only…he looked at her closer. She looked more relaxed than he remembered seeing her before. Happy. So did David, who stood just a little behind her, dressed in a stylish wool winter coat with a matching scarf and leather gloves.

He was different from Duke. He was different than

Evan had been. But he was a nice guy, a stable guy, who had made his mother happy. Duke went forward, gave his mom a hug and then held out his hand to David. "Glad you could make it. Wasn't sure you would with the forecast."

"We left this morning to get ahead of it, like you suggested. Hope you don't mind having us an extra day." Helen looked cautiously hopeful, and Duke realized he hadn't hidden his feelings very well.

"Of course I don't mind."

"I'm glad we got here when we did," David said, unbuttoning his coat. "We hit the first flurries as we came through town."

Quinn, who'd said nothing to this point, stepped in. "Carrie's out doing one last check, but she won't be long. I'm going to finish up here and pick up Amber from day care before it gets too hairy, if that's okay."

"Sure…" Duke only half heard what Quinn had said at the end, but then it suddenly came clear. "Wait, what did you say about Carrie?"

"She wanted to check the herd one last time before the storm. Went out on Sage about thirty minutes ago. The pasture's close, Duke. She'll be back any moment."

"You let her go out there alone?" Fear pummeled his heart, along with anger at Quinn. What on earth were they thinking? "Knowing there's a storm coming?"

Quinn frowned. "She's your foreman, Duke. Have a little faith she knows what she's doing. She's been at this job a long time. She wouldn't go out if she thought she was in danger."

Duke wasn't so sure.

"I'm taking out Badger and going to find her."

"Right. And then I'll have to worry about both of you

being out there." Quinn sighed. "Damn." He checked his watch. Looked out the window.

The radio at his hip crackled.

"Quinn, you there?"

Lacey had come to the foyer. They were all clustered there now while Quinn picked up the radio and answered. "I'm here. You'd best come in, Carrie."

"I've got a dead heifer. Damn coyote's been here and there's just enough snow up here that I've got his tracks."

"Don't go after him, Carrie. That storm's on its way in and you need to get back here."

"Fifteen minutes. I haven't been this close before. I promise. Fifteen minutes."

"Carrie…"

"I've got the rifle. Don't worry. Just…don't tell Duke."

Duke grabbed the radio from Quinn's hand. "Too late."

There was a pause.

"Carrie, get your ass back here. That's an order."

"I have to try," she argued. "We can't afford to lose any more."

What he wanted to say was *I can't afford to lose you.* Instead he barked into the radio, "Don't be stupid!"

"Over, Duke." Her voice was harsh over the slightly staticky connection. "And out."

Duke swore.

Helen's eyes widened and Quinn let out a hefty sigh. "Cats and dogs, you two. I swear. I'd bang your heads together if I thought it would do any good."

"Well, she won't listen to me, that's clear," Duke snapped, handing back the radio. "Maybe you can talk some sense into her while I get dressed."

"Duke, you can't go out there. At least she's familiar with the land…."

Duke pulled on wool socks as he spoke. "I've been riding this land for two months now. Just about every day. I'm not as unfamiliar as you'd think."

"At least take one of the quads. I'll take the other one. The headlights will help if it starts to snow."

"You need to get your daughter."

Lacey stepped up. "Bring her here. We'll watch her."

Duke shoved a heavy hat on his head and pulled out thick gloves. "Go, Quinn. Your kid comes first."

Just as his did.

Hard little snowflakes stung his skin as he crossed to the shed where the quads were kept. He'd filled both with gas and backed his out when Quinn jogged up beside him. "What the hell are you doing?" Duke shouted over the sound of the engine.

"Kailey's going to pick up Amber and bring her here. I'm coming with you."

Duke nodded shortly. He wasn't about to argue. Within two minutes they were on the dirt paths heading to the pasture.

The snow wasn't heavy yet, but the raw feeling in the air and the icy sting to the pellets told Duke it was going to be a doozy when it hit. When they reached the crossroad, Duke pulled up beside Quinn and idled for a second.

"Let's take the perimeter, meet at the northwest corner," he shouted. "Then we'll circle back to here. You find her, you call on the radio."

Quinn nodded, gestured to his left, indicating he'd go in that direction. Duke gunned the engine and headed straight down the path along the east side of the pasture.

He drove for several minutes and saw no sign of her.

Panic started to settle around his heart, but he pushed it away. He had to stay focused. Not let himself get emotionally involved in the situation and let those feelings cloud his judgment. That could wait until later. Because right now the snow was falling heavier and he could only see the dark, hulking shapes of the trees beyond, not the detail now. They had to find her, and soon.

He slowed, stopped for a few seconds and carefully took in the detail around him, looking for any sign that she'd been there. It was only when the engine was quieter that he heard it, and he jumped. The sharp report of a rifle echoing down the valley.

He closed his eyes, searching for the source of the sound, but with the closeness of the weather pressing around him and his partial deafness, he couldn't get a good read on it. Damn it! He turned off the engine to get rid of the noise. "Carrie?" he yelled into the whiteness. "Carrie?"

Nothing.

The shot had definitely come from ahead of him somewhere, so he started the quad again and inched forward, scanning the tree line. After a few hundred yards he saw hoofprints, but they were being covered rapidly by the white flakes. He sped up and followed them as best he could—into the stand of evergreens toward the creek.

The prints suddenly stretched out, uneven and wide as they zigzagged along the edge of the trees. The creek rushed by as he followed the trail, his heart beating hard against his chest. "Carrie!" he called out again, and he heard a reply.

He instantly stopped the quad and listened. "Carrie!"

"Over here!"

The shout echoed along the little valley, but Duke

cursed. The snow was thicker now. He couldn't see the hoofprints anymore, and his disability distorted the source of the sound. Dammit. He'd never felt so helpless, so useless.

He scanned the tree line, hoping to catch a glimpse of her. Why was it everything in his life lately seemed to be out of his control? He slammed his hand down on the handlebars, for the first time truly cursing the odd twist of fate that had put him in harm's way that day. If he hadn't been hurt, he'd be able to hear her voice clearly right now.

"Carrie!"

There was an answering shout, but it sounded disembodied in the hush of snowfall, not loud enough for him to discern words or location.

The radio crackled to life in his hand—a sound that brought with it huge relief. "Duke?" Her sweet voice was clear and he swallowed thickly.

He picked up the radio. "Carrie, I can't see you. I can't hear where you're coming from."

"I'm next to the creek, I can't be too far ahead of you. I heard you calling."

"I'll follow the creek…"

"Be careful. The bank's not as stable as I thought. Sage slipped and threw me."

At least half a dozen curse words slid through his brain, fueled by fear. "Are you okay?"

"Winded, but okay. Cold."

"I'm coming, sweetheart. Tell me when you see headlights." He paused and then spoke again. "Quinn, you getting this?"

"Loud and clear."

"I'm on the east side, not far from the top corner."

"On my way."

Duke moved forward, foot by foot, the lights from the front of the ATV slashing through the swirling snow.

He saw Sage first, standing at the top of the knoll, reins dangling. He slowed and then killed the engine on the quad, sliding off the bike and easing his way toward the horse. "Hey, girl," he said, down low, hoping she wasn't skittish or lame after her upset. Sage butted her head against his hand, and he patted her nose briefly before grabbing the reins and leading her to the quad, where he tied her before setting out for the creek bank.

"Carrie?"

"Over here!"

Her voice was close, and Duke forced himself to take slow and measured steps. They sure didn't need both of them going for a header today. And with the weather closing in rapidly, he was well aware that time was of the essence.

"Keep shouting," he called out.

Instead of shouting, she whistled, which made him smile as he picked his way over the ground. It wasn't long until he found her, leaned up against a spruce tree, her body huddled against the cold. She was wet from the creek, which hadn't quite frozen over yet—he could see the dark splotches of water and dirt on her jeans and jacket. He rushed to her then, kneeling beside her as her teeth chattered.

"I got him," she said, her voice shaking.

The coyote. Right now Duke couldn't care less about any coyote or heifer or anything other than her. "Are you hurt?" He cupped her face in his hands. "Is the baby okay?"

"I landed on my hip and arm," she said, eyes wide. "I don't think anything's broken, just bruised." She met his gaze. "Otherwise I think I'm fine, Duke. Truly."

He gathered her in his arms and held on tight.

Quinn arrived on the other quad. When he reached them on the creek bank, he let out a whistle. "Okay, you two. You can make up at home. Let's get out of here."

Duke pulled back and looked into her eyes. He'd never been so afraid in his life, he realized. Now that she was in front of him, and in his arms, he let the feelings in that he'd had to hold at bay while searching for her. Anger. Fear. Love.

"Don't ever do something like that again! You scared the hell out of me!"

"I didn't mean to upset you...."

Quinn's voice interrupted impatiently. "Can we table this until later? The storm's really settling in and we've got some ground to cover."

Duke nodded, knowing he had a lot to say and now was not the right time or place for it. He picked her up in his arms, adjusted her weight and began making the trek back to the quads and her horse.

"I can walk," she protested.

"Until I know you and the baby are okay, I'm carrying you. Got it?"

Quinn halted abruptly and turned around, his eyes as big as dollar coins. "Did I just hear you right?"

Carrie punched Duke's arm. "Nice going."

"You're pregnant?"

She shrugged, but what struck Duke as comical was Quinn's expression. It was thunderous, while inside not an hour ago he was insisting Duke should trust her to do her job.

Quinn turned back around, muttering something. Duke looked to Carrie for clarification, but she grinned up at him and called out, "Quinn, can you repeat that a little louder for Duke? He's deaf in one ear."

Quinn reached his quad and spun around. "I said, never a dull moment." He looked from Duke to Carrie and threw up his hands. "You two deserve each other."

Duke was inclined to agree.

"Can you drive the quad, do you think? Or are you hurting too much?"

"I'll muddle through. What about Sage?"

"I'll ride her back." He put Carrie gently on the seat of the quad. He looked up at Quinn. "We'll all go together." Then he reached inside his jacket pocket. "Here, put these on. Your gloves are soaked and I don't want you freezing your hands. I wish I had more clothes for you...."

"I'll be fine."

He put his foot in the short stirrup and got up into the saddle, not bothering to take the time to adjust them to a proper length. "Let's go home," he said, and the air was filled with the sound of the engines. Carrie winced as she started out, but once they were rolling she smiled up at him.

She was okay. That was the most important thing. And once she was home and warm and dry, they were going to have a little talk. And she'd listen—to things he should have said a long time ago.

Chapter Sixteen

Carrie ached all over. There was pain in her hip that radiated down her leg every time the quad hit a rut, and her shoulder wasn't feeling so great, either. She was terribly cold, her wet clothes clinging to her as the raw wind penetrated through the material.

And then she looked up at Duke, riding Sage beside her, and a little ball of warmth flickered deep inside. Hearing his voice calling her, hearing it crackle over the radio, was the best sound ever. Seeing him walking over the hard, white earth, coming to her rescue had lit something in her heart that she'd never felt before. It wasn't just seeing him, though that was wonderful. It was a deep-down knowing that he'd come for her. When the chips were down, he'd come for her.

She wasn't used to being a damsel in distress. And she rather hoped it would be a long time before she found herself in such a position again. But it was incredible to realize that she could rely on Duke.

The man who'd ridden out in a storm to find her? That was the real Duke. And that was why she'd fallen in love with him in the first place. He would do the right thing when the chips were down. And if he didn't know how, he'd learn. Just like he'd been learning at the ranch.

For the first time in a very long time, she had faith in someone other than herself.

When the long, rectangular shape of the barn came into view, Carrie nearly wept with joy. They parked the quads in the shed while Duke took Sage to the barn. Quinn helped Carrie off the bike, held her steady.

"You gave us a scare," he said, pulling her close. "I'm with Duke on this one. Don't do it again."

She nodded against the cold front of his jacket.

"You were supposed to go get Amber." Carrie stared up at him. "You didn't because you came looking for me. You shouldn't be driving in this now, Quinn! Oh, God, I'm sorry."

"Amber's hopefully snug as a bug in the house. I called Kailey to get her and bring her back here. Kailey's probably back home already." He grinned. "That fool would have set out alone to get you, you know. I couldn't let him do that."

Duke would have gone out to find her anyway. She was at once thrilled and embarrassed. She should have listened to Quinn. Saved chasing that damned coyote for another day. Her stubbornness had put them all in danger.

"So you two are having a kid. Fast work."

She blushed even as she shivered. "Yeah. Accidental, in case you didn't guess that already."

The grin slid from Quinn's face. "Do me a favor, Carrie. Don't waste time being stupid about things that don't really matter. If you have a chance at happiness, grab at it with both hands. Because you don't know how long it'll last."

Carrie's eyes welled up. "Duly noted, boss."

"I'm going to go check on Amber. I see Duke coming across the yard. Good luck. By the look on his face, you're gonna need it."

Duke stomped snow off his boots as he entered the shed. Carrie expected to be verbally blasted now that they were alone, but Duke merely looked at her expectantly. "Sage is warm and fed, and I'll check her again later. She doesn't appear to be lame, just spooked. Now it's time to get you cleaned up and into some dry things."

"I thought you'd want to talk."

His gaze locked with hers. "Oh, I do," he promised. "But not now. You're cold and wet and need to get warmed up." He gave her a warning look. "You're not going to fight me on this, are you?"

She smiled a little. "Not today. I'm freezing. And I ache all over."

"Come on, then."

They locked up and were halfway to the house when she stepped in a dip and cried out. Duke was right beside her, and before she could protest he'd scooped her into his arms again.

"I feel stupid," she said as he took long strides toward the front steps. "You don't need to carry me. People will talk."

"Like I care," he retorted, stomping up the wooden steps. To her surprise, the door opened and Lacey stood to the side, letting them in.

Duke, thankfully, put her down. Gently.

"Thanks, Lacey," Duke said, pulling off his hat and gloves. He turned his attention to Carrie. The cold had really set in now and she shook all over, so badly that she was having trouble working the zipper on her jacket. Duke did it for her, carefully pushing the coat off her shoulders. He took off her hat and she knew her hair had to be sticking up all over, and then he helped her sit on the steps and pulled off her boots.

"Mom's up running a bath for her," Lacey said quietly.

Carrie looked at Lacey, startled by this bit of news. "Your mom? She's here?"

Duke put down the second boot. "She and David arrived just before I went out after you."

His family Christmas was really happening, then. Carrie wasn't quite sure where she fit in everything. Quinn knew about the baby now, but no one else. She wasn't sure where she and Duke stood, and yet she wanted desperately to be a part of things, too.

"I don't have any clothes to wear," she said dumbly, the inane comment the only thing she could think off amid the turmoil that was churning inside her. If Duke and Quinn hadn't come when they had…

"The bath's ready" came a soft voice.

"Up we go," Duke said, and picked her up into his arms to make the climb to the upstairs.

Lacey followed. "I brought a pair of yoga pants, Carrie. We're not too far from the same size. I'll get them."

"And I'll get you one of my sweatshirts," Duke promised. He stopped at the top of the stairs. "Mom, this is Carrie. Carrie, my mom, Helen."

Carrie didn't know what to say. This afternoon was getting stranger by the second. But Helen just smiled at her. "I'm sure we'll have lots of chance to talk once you're warmed up, dear. I'll go make you some coffee or tea. Or perhaps Duke has some brandy on hand? That always takes the chill off."

The two choices seemed to be caffeine and alcohol, but Duke stepped in smoothly. "Amber's favorite is hot chocolate. How about that instead?"

"That sounds perfect," Carrie replied, sending him a look of thanks.

"Do you need help with anything?" Helen inquired innocently, but Duke stepped in once again.

"I've got it, Mom."

And with those four words, Helen was sent the clear message: *Yeah, it's like that.*

"I'll just be downstairs, then." With a parting smile, Helen left, followed by Lacey, who dropped off the yoga pants on her way by.

Duke finally put her down and she limped her way into the bathroom. Steam rose up from the bath and flowery scented salts had been added—Helen's? Carrie couldn't imagine Joe having such things around. With tender fingers, Duke unbuttoned her shirt and helped her step out of her jeans. Her shoulder protested when she went to take off the shirt and Duke's fingers were there to help, pushing it off her shoulders and down her arms. She was in her underwear now and slightly embarrassed. Not to mention aware. It wasn't the right time or place, but that didn't stop the awareness of knowing that she was alone with Duke. The man she'd fallen in love with, slept with... The man whose baby she carried.

She tried to reach around and unclasp her bra and pain shot down her arm.

"I've got it," Duke murmured, and he undid the hooks at her back.

More self-conscious than ever, she forced down her panties and went straight to the tub. Duke held out his hand and she took it for balance as she stepped over the side and into the blissful heat of the water.

She sat down and let it soak into all the parts of her that ached. Duke perched on the edge of the tub. It wasn't the first time he'd seen her naked, but the context was different. It belied a level of comfort that was more than sexual; a different sort of trust. The kind that gave her a little bit of hope.

"I don't think I thought this through." She smiled up at him. "I'm wounded and naked. I can't run away from you here."

He chuckled. "I thought of that. But when we talk I don't want you at a disadvantage. I want us to be equal. No one in a position of power."

Her heart constricted at the honesty in his eyes. "That sounds like a good place to start," she answered.

"Carrie...you're sure everything's okay with the baby?" Worry shadowed his eyes. "You took quite a fall."

She nodded. "I rolled and landed on my side. I don't have any cramping or anything. I'm just sore in a few spots. But after the storm, I'll follow up with the doctor if you want."

"Never a bad thing to have peace of mind," he agreed. "I'll let you relax now, and meet you downstairs, okay?"

She nodded, but as he reached the door she spoke. "Duke?"

"Yeah?" He turned around.

"I'm sorry I scared you. Sorry I didn't listen. The coyote issue has been nagging at me all fall. I think I felt like if I could solve this, maybe the rest of my life would start coming together. It sounds so stupid when I put it like that...."

"No, it doesn't," he replied. "And as long as you're okay, that's all that matters."

He shut the door with a click, and she sank farther down into the hot water.

THE YOGA PANTS were a perfect fit, and Duke's army sweatshirt was big and cozy. Carrie wrapped her hair into an impromptu bun with an elastic and limped her way down the stairs. The hot water had helped ease some of the stiffness and definitely warmed her up, but she was very aware that she'd be sporting bruises by the morning.

The kitchen smelled delightful, like tomatoes and garlic and pasta. Helen stirred something on the stove and Lacey was washing up a few dishes. Quinn sat in the living room talking to a man Carrie didn't recognize, with Amber curled up in his arms, sleeping. Duke was on the other side of Quinn, one ankle crossed over his knee, relaxing while the fire snapped and crackled in the fireplace.

He noticed her standing there and smiled. "Better?" he asked.

"Much," she answered, smiling back shyly. "Thanks for the shirt."

"Carrie, this is David, my mom's husband." He introduced the other man, who instantly stood to shake her hand.

"I'm glad you both could make it," Carrie offered. "Duke was pretty excited about having you here for the holiday."

"So's Helen," David remarked. "Though it's a shame Rylan didn't make it before the storm."

"There's still time," she said hopefully.

"We can always hope," Duke replied.

"Cocoa's ready," Helen called out.

It was surreal, being in the midst of a big familial gathering. Even more so because Carrie knew things hadn't always been easy in Duke's family. She accepted a cup of cocoa and took a sip. "Oh, this isn't the powdered stuff!" she exclaimed, looking at Duke's mother.

"Milk, cocoa and sugar. Easy as anything and way better than the bought stuff."

"Thank you." She smiled at Helen. "For running the bath and everything. You, too, Lacey," she added, looking over toward the sink. "The pants are perfect."

"You're welcome."

Duke accepted a cup of cocoa and then touched her arm. "Can we go to the office to talk for a few minutes?"

Nerves bubbled in her stomach. A half hour earlier she'd been standing naked in the bathroom in front of him. Things were so not over between them, and she was scared. There was so much at stake. Duke's future, her future, the future of Crooked Valley...and most important of all, the future of their child.

A few minutes? She doubted this could all be solved in a few minutes, but she nodded anyway.

They went down the hall and into the office. The window faced the front of the yard, and it was snowing so hard now Carrie couldn't see past the posts of the veranda. She shivered as she thought about the cattle being outside, but knew their winter coats and instinct to take shelter would see them through. Duke shut the door behind them and her pulse took an anxious leap.

She turned to face him, expecting some sort of reprimand for putting herself in danger, but instead he just stepped forward and wrapped his arms around her, pulling her close to his chest.

"You scared me so bad," he murmured against her hair.

Her eyes stung. "I'm sorry," she replied, her voice thick. "I was so sure I had time. And I would have, if the bank had held and Sage hadn't spooked. I never meant to worry you, Duke."

"I should have gone with you. Quinn should have…"

"Quinn and I both agreed. Don't blame him."

"I don't," Duke answered. "I blame myself."

Carrie lifted her head and pushed away a bit so she could meet his gaze. "Yourself? You didn't do anything wrong! You found me, for God's sake. What do you have to blame yourself for?"

He lifted his hand and placed it on her cheek. "I didn't say the things I should have said. I did things wrong and then left you to just…deal. I forgot that we needed to be working as a team. I let you down, Carrie."

He really thought this was his fault? "Hey," she argued, "I promised I wouldn't take chances, and I was so full of myself and my need to prove things to you that I broke that promise." She reached up and squeezed the fingers that lay against her cheek. "My stupid pride," she said clearly. "Pride and fear."

"Well, next time can we not get caught up in all that pride of yours and my need to be right? It might make things a bit easier. And definitely less stressful for everyone involved."

"Next time?" She frowned.

"Yes, next time. I'm staying on at Crooked Valley."

His words sent a ray of happiness to her heart, but also a thread of apprehension. The ranch needed him, and if he stayed, her job would be secure. Her baby would have a father. And yet…she knew it had to be for the right reasons.

He led her to a chair and she sat while he pulled another one close for himself. He sat, too, reached out and took her hands in his. "I want you to know I heard what you said about me staying out of duty and you're right.

But I can't just leave it out of my decision, because my sense of duty is part of who I am. If I left here, knowing what I'd left behind, I wouldn't be happy. And yes, part of that would be because I would feel I'd failed in my duty. Not just my duty to you, or our child. But the duty to follow my heart."

His gray eyes held her captive as he spoke, his strong hands holding hers tightly, as if afraid if he didn't she'd disappear.

"When I was wounded, I told myself that my hearing was no big deal. I still had all my arms and legs. I could still hear, I just had to make adjustments. But I was lying to myself, Carrie. It wasn't about the hearing. It was about the loss of control of my own life. I felt like I wasn't in charge anymore. Like I was a playing piece being moved around on a board but I didn't know what the game was. Today, when I was trying to find you, I was so angry at the twist of fate that took my hearing because if I had it I'd be able to find you. And then I realized something really, really amazing. If I hadn't lost my hearing, I wouldn't have come back to Crooked Valley. And I wouldn't have found you. And that would have been the worst tragedy of all."

She swallowed against the tears in her throat. "Duke…"

"I've come to love the ranch. I love being outdoors, doing something new every day, working with the animals, working with the staff… I like it here. I know I have a lot to learn but I'd like to learn it. As much as I hate to admit it, my grandfather might have been right all along. This is where I belong. Crooked Valley should be in the family."

She was glad he'd found a connection to the place Joe had loved so deeply.

"But that's not why I'm staying. How can I leave knowing my son or daughter is here? I lost my dad when I was so young and had to grow up without him. I didn't have a choice then, but I do now. I'm going to be a dad to this baby, Carrie. I promise."

She looked down into her lap. He was saying so many good and right things, she should be happy. Instead her heart ached because she'd fallen in love with him weeks ago and he still hadn't said the words to let her know he felt the same. She bit down on her lower lip to keep it from wobbling. His love was the only Christmas gift she wanted.

"Carrie, look at me," he said softly, and she looked up. Her heart instantly constricted as she saw a film of moisture in his eyes.

"I know you think that it's all about duty for me, but that isn't the reason I'm staying. I love you, Carrie. I think I told myself what I was feeling was affection, lust, whatever, to deny what I really felt. But it's love. I know it because when I heard your voice over the radio today I've never been so afraid of losing someone in my whole life. I'd love you if there was no Crooked Valley. I'd love you if there was no baby, though it might have taken me longer to get here." He smiled at her tenderly. "I think I knew that first night when I held you in my arms. Life as I knew it changed."

Her lip wobbled anyway. "For me, too."

"That's good to hear. I was kind of hoping you were with me on the love thing."

She nodded, and the tears in her eyes splashed over her lashes, trickling down her cheeks. "I was. I am." She took in a shaky breath. "I fell in love with you and was sure you didn't feel the same."

"Don't cry," he whispered, letting go of her hands

and wiping away the moisture with his thumbs. "No more crying. We're going to do this thing together, got it? All of it. You, me, our baby, Crooked Valley—we're going to be a family."

She hiccuped out a small laugh. "You're taking this boss thing a little seriously," she teased, while a bubble of joy cautiously rose within her. "Are you still issuing orders, soldier?"

He shook his head, a smile quirking up the corner of his mouth. "I've learned you don't take orders well," he replied. His face turned more serious. "And you're not in my chain of command, sweetheart. If you say yes, it's a partnership all the way."

Her pulse thrummed at the implication. "If I say yes to what?"

"Going on this journey with me. Building a life with me." He leaned forward, and it felt as though her heart was surrounded by tiny little butterflies as he touched his forehead to hers. "Marrying me."

She swallowed, her throat so thick with emotion she could only nod a little while her lips opened but no sound came out.

He leaned back a little so he could look into her face, and she knew she'd never seen anyone look at her that way before. As if she was the center of everything. Loved. Cherished.

"I couldn't hear you," he murmured, and she melted.

"Yes," she said clearly. "Yes. To all of it."

His fingers closed over her wrist and he tugged her off the chair and into his lap, holding her close. "That's a relief!" His words came out in a rush. "I wasn't sure I'd say it right. I have a habit of saying the wrong thing...."

"You always come around in the end," she replied, kissing his cheek, curling into his embrace.

They sat that way for a few minutes when Carrie lifted her head. "Duke? What about Crooked Valley? I know you said you're staying, but what about Lacey's and Rylan's shares? What are you going to do about that?"

He frowned. "I'm not sure, but there's still time. I'll figure it out."

He said it with such confidence that she believed him.

Chapter Seventeen

Duke held Carrie's hand firmly in his own when they left the office. They entered the kitchen and discovered it empty; everyone was sitting in the living room, enjoying the fire. Amber was awake now, playing Chutes and Ladders with her dad in the middle of the floor. Someone had turned on the Christmas tree lights, and the colorful glow plus the flickering fire made things perfectly festive.

Duke met Quinn's gaze, saw Quinn's eyes drop to where Duke's hand was joined with Carrie's and watched as a smile spread on his manager's face.

"I'll be damned," Quinn said, chuckling.

"Daddy! That's a dollar in the swear jar!" Amber's hand paused on her playing piece as she looked up with a frown.

Everyone laughed at Quinn being brought to task by his daughter, her defiant lips at odds with her sweet, curly, blond pigtails. But it also drew their attention to Duke and Carrie, standing in the middle of the arch leading into the room.

"I think my big brother might have an announcement," Lacey said, putting her cocoa mug down on the table.

Duke was used to being in difficult positions, but

facing his family at Christmas and talking about feelings was more than a bit scary. Then Carrie turned her head, looked up at him and smiled encouragingly and the words just came.

"I just asked Carrie to marry me," he said, not looking away from her gorgeous eyes. "And thank God, she said yes."

He swore to himself then and there that he'd work every day to make sure she always looked at him the way she was looking at him right now. With love and trust and faith. He'd do everything in his power to make sure he didn't break with those values.

A chorus of surprise rose from the group, with Amber jumping up from her blocks and clapping her hands. "Will you get to wear a dress and everything?"

Carrie nodded, a blush lighting her cheeks. He loved it when she blushed like that.

Duke let go of her hand briefly, squeezing her fingers first and giving her a questioning nod. She nodded back, so he went to where his mother was sitting and knelt beside her chair.

"Mom, I know we haven't been that close in recent years, but I'd like that to change. And so I want to tell you first. You're going to be a grandmother."

Her lips dropped open in surprise. There was no question that the pregnancy was unplanned. He discovered he didn't need his mother's approval, but he wanted it just the same and he attempted to explain. "I know it feels rushed, but we…we just fell fast and hard. I love her."

She patted his hand, a wistful smile on her lips. "It was like that for your father and me, too. I think I knew from the moment he asked me to dance. It seems you're still your father's son," she joked tenderly.

Duke looked up at Carrie, his heart so full he wasn't sure he could stand it.

Helen spoke again. "Duke, as long as you're happy, I'm happy. That's all a mother ever wants for her kids."

"I am. Very."

Helen smiled at Carrie. "Congratulations, then, and welcome to the family, dear."

Lacey had remained fairly quiet during the whole announcement thing, but David filled the gap of silence smoothly. "I think this calls for a toast or something. Is there any of that cocoa left?"

The cocoa was reheated and everyone had a little in their mugs preparing to toast when the front door opened with a gust of wind and slammed shut again.

Duke went to the hall and stared at the sight before him—a tall man shaking the snow off his cowboy hat.

"Rylan!"

Rylan looked up, a sideways grin lighting his face. "Merry Christmas, bro," he said.

"Duke? Who is it?"

Carrie voiced the question behind him. Duke reached back for her hand and pulled her forward, wrapping his arm around her shoulder. "Carrie, meet my little brother Rylan. Rylan—meet the woman who's going to make an honest man out of me and make you an uncle."

The blank look on Rylan's face made Duke laugh, and a feeling of perfect contentment swept over him.

Carrie looked up at him and grinned. "You got your big family Christmas after all."

"More than I ever dreamed," Duke replied.

* * * * *

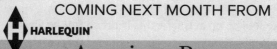

REQUEST YOUR FREE BOOKS!
2 FREE NOVELS PLUS 2 FREE GIFTS!

HARLEQUIN®

American ★ Romance®

LOVE, HOME & HAPPINESS

YES! Please send me 2 FREE Harlequin® American Romance® novels and my 2 FREE gifts (gifts are worth about $10). After receiving them, if I don't wish to receive any more books, I can return the shipping statement marked "cancel." If I don't cancel, I will receive 4 brand-new novels every month and be billed just $4.74 per book in the U.S. or $5.24 per book in Canada. That's a savings of at least 14% off the cover price! It's quite a bargain! Shipping and handling is just 50¢ per book in the U.S. and 75¢ per book in Canada.* I understand that accepting the 2 free books and gifts places me under no obligation to buy anything. I can always return a shipment and cancel at any time. Even if I never buy another book, the two free books and gifts are mine to keep forever.

154/354 HDN F4YN

Name _____ (PLEASE PRINT) _____

Address _____ Apt. #

City _____ State/Prov. _____ Zip/Postal Code

Signature (if under 18, a parent or guardian must sign)

Mail to the **Harlequin® Reader Service:**
IN U.S.A.: P.O. Box 1867, Buffalo, NY 14240-1867
IN CANADA: P.O. Box 609, Fort Erie, Ontario L2A 5X3

Want to try two free books from another line?
Call 1-800-873-8635 or visit www.ReaderService.com.

* Terms and prices subject to change without notice. Prices do not include applicable taxes. Sales tax applicable in N.Y. Canadian residents will be charged applicable taxes. Offer not valid in Quebec. This offer is limited to one order per household. Not valid for current subscribers to Harlequin American Romance books. All orders subject to credit approval. Credit or debit balances in a customer's account(s) may be offset by any other outstanding balance owed by or to the customer. Please allow 4 to 6 weeks for delivery. Offer available while quantities last.

Your Privacy—The Harlequin® Reader Service is committed to protecting your privacy. Our Privacy Policy is available online at www.ReaderService.com or upon request from the Harlequin Reader Service.

We make a portion of our mailing list available to reputable third parties that offer products we believe may interest you. If you prefer that we not exchange your name with third parties, or if you wish to clarify or modify your communication preferences, please visit us at www.ReaderService.com/consumerchoice or write to us at Harlequin Reader Service Preference Service, P.O. Box 9062, Buffalo, NY 14269. Include your complete name and address.

HAR13R

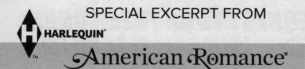
*Looking for more all-American romances like the one
you just read? Read on for an excerpt from
Cathy Gillen Thacker's LONE STAR CHRISTMAS
from her **McCABE MULTIPLES** miniseries!*

Nash Echols dropped a fresh-cut Christmas tree onto the
bed of a flatbed truck. He watched as a luxuriously outfit-
ted red SUV tore through the late November gloom and
came to an abrupt stop on the old logging trail.

"Well, here comes trouble," he murmured, when the
driver door opened and two equally fancy peacock-blue
boots hit the running board.

His glance moved upward, taking in every elegant inch
of the cowgirl marching toward him. He guessed the sassy
spitfire to be in her early thirties, like him. She glared while
she moved, her hands clapped over her ears to shut out the
concurrent whine of a dozen power saws.

Nash lifted a leather-gloved hand.

One by one his crew stopped, until the Texas mountain-
side was eerily quiet, and only the smell of fresh-cut pine
hung in the air. And still the determined woman advanced,
chin-length dark brown curls framing her even lovelier face.

He eased off his hard hat and ear protectors.

Indignant color highlighting her delicately sculpted
cheeks, she stopped just short of him and propped her hands
on her slender denim-clad hips. "You're killing me, using
all those chain saws at once!" Her aqua-blue eyes narrowed.
"You know that, don't you?"

Actually, Nash hadn't.

Her chin lifted another notch. *"You have to stop!"*

At that, he couldn't help but laugh. It was one thing for this little lady to pay him an unannounced visit, another for her to try to shut him down. "Says who?" he challenged right back.

She angled her thumb at her sternum, unwittingly drawing his glance to her full, luscious breasts beneath the fitted red velvet Western shirt, visible beneath her open wool coat. "Says me!"

"And you are?"

"Callie McCabe-Grimes."

Of course she was from one of the most famous and powerful clans in the Lone Star State. He should have figured that out from the moment she'd barged onto his property.

Nash indicated the stacks of freshly cut Christmas trees around them, aware the last thing he needed in his life was another person not into celebrating the holidays. "Sure that's not Grinch?"

Look for LONE STAR CHRISTMAS
by Cathy Gillen Thacker from the
***McCABE MULTIPLES** miniseries from*
Harlequin American Romance.

Available December 2014
wherever books and ebooks are sold.

www.Harlequin.com